Prologue

Hannah followed Jen and Kulvita into the coffee bar. Hannah didn't know much about the two girls, only that they'd just survived their very first English lecture together, which was all she needed to know right now. Kulvita strode towards the counter. Hannah hung back a little with Jen, looking around, taking everything in.

There was a crowd of students, all a bit younger than her, but probably second or third years, shrieking and laughing at the large centre table. A scarily studious-looking girl was sitting by the far window peering at her laptop and – oh God, no, not possible!

Hannah froze as she saw a guy sitting alone at a corner table, a mug, folder and pile of books in front of him. He was reading, his head down so she hadn't got a clear view, but Hannah knew it was him. She knew, but her mind refused to accept it.

He couldn't be here. Fate, coincidence or whatever, couldn't have brought him to the same university at the same time. It had been five years. That part of her life was over, finished. It couldn't have followed her here, it just couldn't.

Her heart was thumping so hard she was sure everyone could hear it. She'd always known she might bump into one of the old crowd again, even though she'd made it almost impossible for anyone to get in touch, but she couldn't handle this, no way. If it was Clare or Mica or even Jackie sitting there, she might be able to cope, but not him. Why did it have to be him? She tried to breathe deeply, to think. OK, he couldn't have known she was coming here. This couldn't be deliberate. It had to be coincidence but it didn't make it any better.

'Do you know him?' Jen said, as Hannah continued to stare.

She had to get out of here before he looked up, before he saw her.

'Yeah, sort of,' Hannah muttered, backing away, knowing she was acting like a total freak. 'You go ahead, I'll catch up later.'

Jen looked at her, puzzled, before moving to join Kulvita in the queue. The movement, the flash of Jen's bright-red top, must have caught his

Other books by Sandra Glover

Sandra Glover

Northumberland County Council	
3 0132 02118531 4	
Askews & Holts	Jul-2012
JF	£6.99
	.

ANDERSEN PRESS LONDON

First published in 2011 by
ANDERSEN PRESS LIMITED
20 Vauxhall Bridge Road, London SW1V 2SA
www.andersenpress.co.uk
www.sandraglover.co.uk

British Library Cataloguing in Publication Data available.

ISBN 978 184 270 994 8

Printed and bound in Great Britain by CPI Bookmarque,
Croydon CR0 4TD

attention. Before Hannah could back towards the door, he looked up. It killed any possible doubt that it was him even before he stood, pushing his chair back so quickly it almost toppled over.

'Hannah!' he said, loud enough for the whole coffee bar to hear.

She tried to stop herself shaking as everyone's eyes turned towards her. They didn't know, she reminded herself, they didn't know. To them this was just two old friends bumping into each other, a momentary diversion. People were already starting to look away, turning their attention back to their own friends.

It was too late to move. He'd almost reached her. It was like that moment that's supposed to happen just before you die, when everything comes rushing back, your life flashing before you. Only this wasn't her whole life, just the worst part. The part she'd spent five years, in and out of counselling, trying to forget; the fallout from that bloody party back when she was just sixteen.

1

'Hannah!'

The sound of her name crashed into her head, echoing over and over. The tone of that single word was high-pitched and hysterical, like the house was on fire or something. Hannah opened her eyes but she couldn't see much, only the blurred outlines of her bedroom. There were no flames, no smell of smoke. What was going on?

She tried to turn but the slightest movement set her stomach lurching. So she lay still again although somehow the movement went on, as if her bed was bouncing on a choppy sea. Up and down, up and down. Waves rolled round her body, churning up memories, nightmares, things that couldn't be real. Except she knew they were.

'Hannah!'

Forcing her eyes open a bit further, Hannah fixed them on the blur of the digital display and tried to make the numbers come into focus. There was a one and a four and – oh, no – 14:07!

'Hannah!'

The time, her name being called again, told her everything she really didn't want to know. It was her mother shouting. They were back. It was Sunday afternoon already – oh shit! Hannah let her eyelids drop, not wanting to dwell on the time, or the overturned wine bottle on the floor. She didn't want to see the discarded clothes, the reminders; the evidence.

It was easy enough to close her eyes to the reddish-brown stains on the pale-blue carpet. But she couldn't close her nose to the stale, sickly, suffocating smells that crept down her burning throat, making her retch. And she couldn't close her ears to the sound of her name still being called.

Dad was shouting now. Behind his voice, deep and insistent, came a hazy confusion of other sounds. She could hear doors slamming, furniture scraping, pots clattering and glass tinkling. Kyra was down there too, yelping, 'Oh my gosh,' over and over in her sickly-cute way. They must have picked her up from Gran's on their way back. Oh great, Kyra was just what she absolutely didn't need right now.

Outside, birds were twittering and skittering. A dog was yapping and, somewhere out the back, in the distance, a lawn mower was revving. Why couldn't they be quiet? Why couldn't they all shut up, go away, leave her alone? She needed time to think. No, don't think, don't even start to go there. She squeezed her eyes tightly shut, just wanting to sleep. Sleep forever to make it all go away.

'Hannah, get down here right now!'

Did Dad know what he was asking? She could barely move. She couldn't even lift her head, stretch her fingers or wriggle her toes. She heard two sets of footsteps; Kyra's light ones tripping past, then Mum's stopping outside her room. Hannah sensed, rather than saw, the bedroom door being flung open. She could hear her mum muttering about the mess as she picked her way through the debris and pulled back the curtains. The room was instantly flooded with bright, glaring light that Hannah could see even with her eyes closed.

'It stinks in here,' Mum announced, opening the windows, letting in a rush of hot July air, like a blast from a giant hairdryer. 'Dear God, Hannah! Look at the state of you! Look at your room!'

Instinctively Hannah pulled the duvet round her. She shivered, even though the sunlight was falling directly on the bed. It made her blink as she tried to open her eyes again.

'What's happened to your face?' Mum asked. 'Is that a bruise?'

Hannah put her hand up to the area between her left eye and the top of her cheekbone, which felt all sore and puffy.

'I don't know. I think I might have been rubbing it or fallen or walked into something. I can't remember I was ...'

'Drunk! Too drunk to know what the hell you were doing,' said Mum. 'Oh, Hannah, how could you? I thought we could trust you. It was only supposed to be a few friends!'

'It was,' Hannah managed to say.

Three girls, that's all she'd invited. Three close friends, or what passed for close friends these days, for a gossipy, girly night of pizza, DVDs and a few glasses of wine. She should have known it wouldn't be enough for those three!

Jackie bursting in, laughing, half-pissed already, even though it was barely seven thirty. Stacy clutching two carrier bags, bottles clinking and cans rattling. Clare shuffling in behind Stacy, looking nervous, edgy. Then someone else, a fourth person, someone Hannah hadn't invited. It was Jackie's cousin, Eden, in her tarty, tight top and micro-skirt, strolling into the lounge, picking up the DVDs from the coffee table. Maybe she wasn't staying or maybe she was off to a club later. Girly gatherings weren't really Eden's thing. She only hung around with her younger cousin, Jackie, when she was desperate, or when she fancied causing trouble.

'We won't want these,' Eden said, shoving the DVDs in a drawer, 'but we might need to move some furniture.'

'Why? Hang on — what's going on?'

'Chill, Hannah, I've invited a few lads from school, that's all,' Jackie said, giggling. 'And Eden's tagged along cos her bloke's stood her up again.'

'He didn't stand me up! He's busy, he's working.'

'Whatever,' Jackie drawled.

'Who?' Hannah had asked, cutting across their bickering. 'Who've you invited?'

'Oh, you know,' Jackie said, 'the usual lot from our year: Liam, Ravi and Mica.'

OK, that wasn't too bad.

'And a few from the Sixth Form — Josh but he's off to some boring family thing — oh, and Shane.'

'Shane!'

'Yeah, Shane, why not?' Eden said. 'He won't bring Lucy, will he? She's at her dad's.'

*

'Like I'm supposed to believe that,' her mother was saying, 'like a few girls could make that much mess! Have you seen it, Hannah, have you seen the state of my house? I don't suppose you've been downstairs and bothered to look? Do you even care?'

There were too many questions to even think about answering. Hannah couldn't see Mum clearly but she could imagine the raised, neatly-plucked eyebrows and the blue eyes dulled to grey fury. She could picture the pink patches that flared on Mum's cheeks and round her neck when she was mad.

She should have said no to the party. She should have kicked her so-called friends out, locked the doors and barricaded herself in! She'd tried a few feeble protests but it was hard to say no to Eden and Jackie. Besides, it hadn't been too bad at first. A few lads from school turning up, like Jackie had said. People partying, having fun and there was no sign of Shane. Some mess, sure, but no damage, no serious damage. Then more texts had been sent, word had got round. Shane arrived, alone. Before she could even speak to him, more people started to turn up — the wrong people, exactly the people she'd wanted to avoid.

'Well, I want you downstairs right now, do you understand?' Mum snapped. 'The least you can do is help clear up.'

Hannah raised her head high on the pillow. Mum was standing at the bottom of the bed with an old shirt of Dad's loosely buttoned over her smart cream dress. Her hands were already encased in yellow plastic gloves, ready for action.

'I need to shower,' was all Hannah could say.

'I expect you do! But be quick and you'll have to use ours. The downstairs shower's awash with vomit. And you really, really wouldn't want to go in the house bathroom – not without a bucket of bleach. How could you do this, Hannah, how could you?' her mum asked, storming out without waiting for a reply.

Hannah lay for a moment trying to steady the continual motion of her head and stomach. She tried to force away the nausea, the dizziness, desperately trying to remember exactly what she'd drunk last night. She hadn't drunk much, not at first. But what about later, after things started to go wrong? She remembered going into the kitchen and picking up a bottle, but she wasn't sure about anything after that, until . . . No! She didn't want to think about it. She just wanted it all to go away, wish herself back twenty-four hours.

She eased herself a little further up so her aching back was resting on the pillow. She tried a deep breath, taking in a foul mix of the spilled red wine, her mum's lingering perfume and something musty, mouldy almost. But more intense than any of these was the sudden overpowering smell of *him*. Why hadn't she noticed it before? Had her mum noticed? It was everywhere. It was on her pillow, on her duvet, on her skin, making her retch. She got up and put on a long T-shirt. Her whole body was swaying, reeling and lurching as she tried to wriggle her arms into the short sleeves.

Pulling all the bedclothes off the bed, she bundled them into a tight ball before slowly making her way to her mum's bathroom. Her head was thudding with every step as she skirted her way around empty cans, discarded cigarettes and the scattered books from an overturned bookcase. The mess was worse than she'd thought, worse than she remembered. The carpet was squelching with beer, or at least she hoped it was only beer. There were pictures pulled from the walls and the door to her sister's bedroom was all but ripped off, hanging from a single hinge. When the hell had that happened?

Glimpsing Kyra standing in the middle of her room, turning in slow circles amidst the debris, Hannah tried to hurry past but it was too late. Kyra spotted her, burst out and grabbed Hannah's arm. Her sharp little nails dug in tight.

'Get off me, you freak,' Hannah snapped, kicking out.

Kyra stepped back but she didn't let go. She was small for her age, very thin, but she was strong too. Her muscles toned by endless bloody ballet exercises.

'They've taken my Nintendo!' Kyra yelled, tightening her grip. 'Someone's nicked my Nintendo and my TV and look what they've done to my room!'

Kyra's room, usually all nauseatingly neat fluffy pinkness, was as wrecked as the rest of the house. Her precious ballet certificates had been ripped off the walls. Her clothes, stupid dance CDs, fluffy animals and other ultra-cute-Kyra-stuff were all scattered. Whoever had nicked her Nintendo obviously didn't fancy the pink bunny or the sparkly leotard.

'Get off,' Hannah said, kicking out again, squealing as her bare foot landed on something sharp.

'I'm telling Mum,' Kyra whined.

Her bottom lip was quivering like she was six, not recently turned twelve, but at least she let go of Hannah's arm. Kyra ran off downstairs, whilst Hannah bent to pull out the piece of glass that had wedged in her foot. She rubbed away the blood with her hand then limped off to the shower, before Kyra could come back with Mum. She turned the water on high but kept it very cool.

She let it gush over her face, her hair and her body, letting it wash everything away – only it couldn't. Water couldn't swill away the images of the party that were forcing their way through her brain, whirling in front of her eyes, squeezed shut. Oh God! She pushed her way out of the shower. Grabbing a towel, she wrapped it round her before sinking onto her knees in front of the loo and throwing up.

'Hannah, have you finished in there?'

She flushed the loo by way of an answer. Stretching her right arm, she gripped the edge of the sink. Then she pulled herself unsteadily to her feet and faced herself in the mirror. Her hair was wet, dripping onto her shoulders, looking more brown than blonde. She pushed it back behind her ears, as she leaned forward to examine her eyes. They looked awful! The blueness was all clouded. The whites were streaked with red and the lids were all puffy like she'd been crying.

Had she cried? Had she had time to cry? The area around her left eye was discoloured but it wasn't too bad. Not as bad as the bruise at the top of her right arm. Her tongue felt huge and furry. But when she stuck it out, it looked strangely normal, unlike her lips, which were swollen and sore.

'Hannah!'

She grabbed Mum's foundation from the cabinet and dabbed some on, covering up the worst of the damage. The towel had started to slip so she pulled it round her, as tightly as she could. She knotted it at the top, draped the T-shirt over her shoulders and headed out to face Mum.

'Get dressed and get yourself downstairs,' Mum said.

Mum picked up some of the rubbish from her bedroom and dropped it into a black bin liner, which was almost full. The stench from it made Hannah retch again. She clamped her hand over her mouth and swallowed, fighting back the bile that was gushing up. No way did she want to go downstairs but she didn't have much choice. So she went back to her own room, grabbed some jeans, found a long-sleeved cotton top and got dressed.

Before leaving her room, she picked up the bundle of bedding and scooped all the clothes that were lying on the floor. Taking the whole lot downstairs she put them straight in the washing machine. The sickly-soapy smell of the powder and the whirr of the machine starting up set off the nausea, the dizziness again. She leaned against one of the work surfaces but it didn't help. With every throb of her temple came the images, the memories that wouldn't go away, that wouldn't ever go away.

How had it happened? How had she let it happen and what was she supposed to do? Standing up straight, she paused until she got her balance then headed to the sink. She got a glass of water, took a few sips and pulled her phone from the pocket of her jeans. But what was the point, who could she talk to, who could she tell? No one would believe her and no way could she let Mum and Dad find out.

They'd never understand. They'd say it was her own fault. They'd be so angry – even angrier than they were now. Say nothing, do nothing. Try to act normal, forget it; it was the only way. These things happened – possibly more often than she'd ever imagined. She could cope. She could handle it. She had to.

Still undecided, still clutching the phone, she turned away and headed slowly towards the lounge, where her parents were waiting. Outside the door she stopped. She quickly tapped in a text. What next? Send it? Delete it? Her limbs were aching. She still felt sick and so confused. She couldn't think straight about anything. Her parents were going to kill her. She'd be grounded for ever. But it barely mattered.

'Hannah, will you get in here!'

2

Shane groaned and stretched out on the settee. He rubbed his eyes as he stared at the TV but it didn't help. All he could see was a fuzz of colour, like he had a hangover or something. But it wasn't a hangover – it couldn't be, no way. He hadn't drunk enough for that.

'Shane,' his mum called from the kitchen, 'I hope you haven't got that TV on! You're supposed to be doing your homework.'

'I'll do it in a minute,' he yelled.

He kicked off his trainers, sending bits of dried mud flying everywhere, and pulled his knees up to his chest, muttering in a fair imitation of his mum's voice.

'Do your homework, Shane. Tidy your room, Shane. Don't forget to shower, Shane.'

Why couldn't she leave him alone? Why couldn't she just let him stay in bed? TV was a bit loud though. She was right about that. He should have been more careful, kept it down and made out like he was working. He looked round for the remote. No, it wasn't there. It was probably buried under all his folders scattered across the floor.

Oh bugger, IT was due at the end of last term. He'd absolutely promised to drop it into school this week. Last chance, he'd been told! Like the bloody English, which was supposed to be finished three weeks ago but which he hadn't even started yet. He uncurled, leaned forward and picked up the green folder. He pulled out the thick clump of notes Mrs Perry had given them, groaned and threw them on the floor. Sod it. He'd do it later. He was way too knackered now and no frickin' wonder after last night!

He sniffed, wondering whether he was coming down with a summer cold, then sniffed again. God, was that him? He folded his arms tight across his stomach to stop it gurgling. Oh well, at least there was no one around to moan about the rumbling – or the smells. Dad, workaholic as ever, had gone off to finish some job and Mum was out there in the kitchen making curry of all things! Why couldn't they have a roast on Sunday, like normal people? No wonder his gut was kicking off.

Above the noise of his stomach, he heard the doorbell buzz. Still clutching his middle he curled up again. Mum could answer it. It'd only be old Mrs Yates from next door, anyway. She turned up most Sunday afternoons, hobbling in with her walking stick tap-tapping and her chest wheezing.

If they were really unlucky she'd bring them some rock-hard, home-made scones or squelchy, soggy fruitcake. Even that wouldn't be too bad if she just dumped it and left, but no, she always stayed for a 'little chat'. Then Mum ended up asking her to stay for dinner. Oh joy of bloody joys!

'Well, she's eighty-six,' Mum would say. 'She's not in the best of health and she's on her own, poor thing – unless you count her son who turns up every six months if she's lucky. So you be nice to her, Shane.'

Yeah right, nice as in death by boredom! Nice as in listening to endless stories of how things were different in the good old days! Just thinking about it set him off yawning.

'Please, please, please don't let it be Mrs Yates,' he mumbled, as the yawn faded, 'not now, not today.'

He'd closed his eyes but he opened them again, as he heard someone come into the lounge. Shit, he recognised that perfume! He should do, he'd bloody bought it! So definitely not Mrs Yates.

It was Lucy. What the hell was she doing here? He blinked as she appeared in front of him, hoping he was hallucinating – but no such luck.

'Hey, Lucy!' he said.

'God, you look gross,' Lucy said, kicking a folder out of the way and flopping down beside him. 'What you been doing? No, don't answer that!'

'Er . . . I thought you were still at your dad's.'

'Yeah, I was gonna stay the whole week but . . .'

'You were missing me too much?' he managed to say.

'Sort of. No, course I was. But it was her!'

Not hard to guess who she was talking about. 'Her' meant an endless rant about Lucy's stepmum was going to start. Oh great! Even Mrs Yates's rock cakes and rationing stories would have been better than this. At least Mrs Yates paused to draw breath sometimes. She had to cos of her bronchitis!

'I just can't stand the bitchy old cow,' Lucy was droning. 'I'd have killed her if I'd stayed any longer. Honestly, Shane, she gets worse. I mean, it's obvious she doesn't want me there. Moans and snipes the minute I walk through the door. "Don't leave your bags there, Lucy. Gosh, you've brought a lot – looks like you're staying for a month. Don't think we could put up with each other for that long." Then she giggles and simpers at Dad, like it's supposed to be a joke. Shane, are you listening or what?'

'Yeah, course,' he said, turning to face her.

'Next thing she says is that I've put on weight! I mean, like *she* can talk! She's, like, seriously flabby since she had the twins – stomach on her like a pot-bellied pig. Anyway I haven't put on weight, have I? Do you think I have?'

Yep, definitely – all that comfort eating during exams probably. Crisps, cream cakes and cram-ming – lethal!

'No!' he said. 'No way, Luce, you look great.'

He smiled at her. It wasn't like a total lie. Even with the extra weight Lucy looked well good. Not supermodel slim, like Eden, but definitely not fat and she had totally amazing boobs. He tried not to stare but it was hard not to in that low-cut top she was wearing. They were positively dangling out, right in front of him!

'Anyway, she doesn't give me a bloody minute with Dad on my own. Not that he's got time for me now anyway. Not now they've got the brats who just scream and whine all the bloody time. God, they're the ugliest babies I've ever seen. They take after their mother – all pointy little noses, chubby cheeks and narrow eyes.'

Shane laughed as Lucy blew out her cheeks and squeezed her eyes into what was supposed to be a picture of the twins and their mother. That was what he liked about Lucy. She could always make him laugh, even when he was pissed off.

'Doesn't suit you,' he said, leaning forward to kiss her, 'you could never be ugly no matter how many faces you pull.'

'Uggh,' she said, pushing him away, 'your breath stinks.'

'Thanks!'

'Well it does! Have you started smoking again?'

And this was what he didn't like about her!

'No!' he said.

'Liar!'

'I had a couple last night but I've cleaned my teeth.'

'You need to do them again,' she said. 'I can smell beer too, you been partying or something?'

'Well, yeah,' Shane said, trying not to make eye contact. 'I did go out last night.'

No point lying, she'd find out soon enough. Everyone would be talking about it. Best to tell the truth – or at least part of it – no way could he tell her everything. Not unless he had a death wish.

'Oh,' she said, looking at him, rolling her tongue

over her lips, the way she did when she was about to have a serious go at him. 'Well, I don't suppose you have to stay in all the time just cos I was away.'

Dead right!

'So whose party was it? Anyone I know?'

This was it. This was crunch time, explosion time.

'Hannah's,' he said, holding his stomach as it set off rumbling again.

Instead of the explosion, from either his stomach or Lucy, there was silence. Lucy got up and wandered towards the television. She turned, standing in front of it, hands on hips, looking at him. Then she picked up the remote from underneath one of his folders and turned the sound down before she spoke.

'I didn't know she was having a party,' she said. 'But then I don't suppose she'd tell me, would she? I bet she waited till I went away. Devious cow!'

'It wasn't planned or nothing,' Shane said. 'I got a text from Eden last night.'

'Eden, not Hannah?' Lucy quizzed. 'It was Eden who sent the text?'

'Yeah, Eden,' he said.

He let go of his stomach and clutched his neck instead, trying to hide the blush he could feel burning under his chin. Oh bugger, it was no good. It was already creeping upwards and outwards, spreading round his jaw up to his cheeks. She was sure to notice!

'I didn't know you were that friendly with Eden.'

He shifted on his seat. *Bloody hell, what was this, the bloody inquisition or what?*

'I'm not,' he said. 'She was texting everyone, I reckon. I mean, I wasn't gonna go but you know Eden when she gets an idea in her head! She kept pestering and with you away there was nothing else to do.'

'So you went?'

Oh God! Did he have to spell everything out?

'Yeah, but not till late. It must have been gone ten and I didn't stay long, only about an hour or so, I reckon.'

That at least was true, well, partly, sort of. Maybe he hadn't been too accurate about the timing.

'Was it any good?'

'What?'

'The party, what do you think I meant?'

She was really staring at him now, her deep-brown eyes trying to drill right into his head, looking for clues.

'Yeah, it was all right,' he muttered, 'at first.'

Lucy carried on staring. That was so typical of girls – see them for a couple of weeks and they thought they had exclusive rights. Give them a few months and they were looking at bloody engagement rings.

'Good,' she said. 'Glad you managed to enjoy yourself without me.'

That's why he'd dumped Hannah – the possessive bit, getting all serious. Well that and cos he got together with Lucy, of course, which sort of happened by accident. And now – well things were complicated now, after last night. He still couldn't believe what had happened. What a mess, what a frickin', stupid mess!

'So?' Lucy said, running her fingers through her dark poker-straight hair, shoving it behind her ears. 'What happened?'

'Nothing! Well, it got a bit mad. Why all the questions, anyway?'

'Was Zak there?' she said, like she wanted to draw out every detail.

Before he could answer there was a sharp knock on the lounge door. Yes! Saved, or at least for now. The knock was pointless, as the door was wide-open anyway. But that was Mum for you, pretending to be all subtle. Like she expected him and Lucy to be making out, right there on the floor. Some chance!

'I've made you some coffee,' Mum said, coming in, putting two mugs on the table.

Mum looked at the folders, the scattered notes and his dirty trainers. She gave an exaggerated sniff and winked at Lucy. Then her expression changed.

'Oh, is everything all right, Lucy?' she said. 'You look a bit upset.'

'Her dad's was crap so she came back,' said Shane.

'Don't use words like that, Shane,' his mum said.

Like 'crap' was bad! She'd have a fit if she heard him when he was out with his mates! She'd have a fit about a lot of things, if she knew. Oh well, at least his little trick had worked. At least Lucy had shut up about the bloody party and set off about her dad again.

Straightaway Mum was in there, fussing over her, drawing out all the gory details about her wicked stepmother and the ugly little stepsisters! Lucy snuffling, Mum putting her arm round her, leading her over to a chair! Oh seriously – totally OTT with the sympathy. It wasn't like someone had died! A few months back Mum hadn't even liked Lucy. She'd blamed her for the split with Hannah. Not like it was any of Mum's business.

'Such a lovely girl, Hannah,' she'd gushed, all the time he'd been going out with her, 'such a nice family.'

But now Mum was treating Lucy like a ruddy daughter-in-law. Scary! No surprise though, Mum just loved all the girly talk. It didn't matter who the girl was. She gushed round his brother's wife too, like she'd have been happier with daughters instead of being lumbered with two stinky, noisy lads.

His phone bleeped, making Lucy look towards him again. He pulled it out. Shit! He'd been expecting it, he'd even half worked out his reply but he couldn't do it now, not with Mum and Lucy staring.

'Anil,' he said, snapping the phone shut, putting it away. 'He'll be whinging about me not turning up for footy practice again this morning.'

That sounded believable. Anil, sporty type rather than party type, was always trying to get him back into football and tennis.

'You ought to go,' Mum said, 'you used to love your football.'

'No point, I never get picked anymore.'

'That's because you drink too much and don't go to training,' Mum said. 'You don't even play for the school now.'

'I told you! The Sixth Form don't even have a team any more. No one's got time, there's too much work.'

'Not that I ever see you doing any,' Mum said, looking down at his unopened folders. 'You'll have to get your act together next year or you won't get into university. Have you decided what you're doing next year, Lucy?'

'Not yet, not for definite, I'll wait and see what my GCSEs are like. I should be able to scrape into Sixth Form but I'm not sure I want to. I wouldn't mind getting away from school,' she said, glancing at Shane. 'I've been offered a place at college on that health and beauty course that *Eden's* been doing.'

She stressed the name, Eden, as she looked at Shane again.

'So, like I said, I'll just wait and decide when results come out.'

'That sounds sensible,' said Mum. 'Keep your options open, that's what I'm always telling Shane.'

Shane raised his eyebrows and smiled at Lucy as his mum droned on. But he was wasting his time. Lucy was in mega-sulk mode now. She was looking at his pocket, where he'd put the phone, which was bleeping again. He took it out and had a quick look. People were obviously starting to wake up, sober up. He'd probably be getting texts and calls about the bloody party for the rest of the day, if not the rest of the bloody year. He put the phone on silent before shoving it back in his pocket.

'Anil again?' Lucy asked.

'Er, no, someone else, it was, er, Mica.'

Lucy swigged back the rest of her coffee and stood up.

'You're not going already?' Mum said.

'Yeah, I told my mum I wouldn't be long. I promised I'd clean my room this afternoon.'

Cleaning her room, yeah, right! Shane got up, walked with Lucy to the door and leaned in to kiss her but she turned away.

'Look, it was just a party, OK?' he said.

She didn't believe him, she didn't trust him. Well, so what, it didn't matter. If Lucy dumped him, he'd find someone else. He knew at least two in his own year who were interested. And then there was always – well, no, maybe not. Anyway, it wouldn't come to that. He'd probably get it sorted with Lucy. And if not, well he'd keep his options open, like Mum said. It'd be all right. It always was.

3

Mum was picking up rubbish, loading it into a new black bin liner. Kyra was holding the bin bag open, still moaning about her missing stuff and the state of her room, squeezing out a few tears for added effect. No one could cry to order quite like Kyra! Dad was sweeping up debris but they all stopped when Hannah finally walked in.

'You took your time,' Dad snarled.

He didn't seem to notice the bruise so maybe the foundation had worked or maybe he just didn't care. He was too busy worrying about the mess.

'Sorry.'

Hannah tried to make the single word sound genuine and apologetic. There was no point winding him up more than he already was. She couldn't cope with a full-blown row. She felt so ill she couldn't cope with anything really but she had to try.

'Sorry?' he said, looking round the room, 'sorry hardly starts to cover it, does it? Are you going to tell us what happened?'

She'd have to say something. She'd have to tell them part of it at least. Something, anything to make it sound as if she was being helpful and co-operative but it was difficult to think, hard to focus, impossible to know what to say. Hannah glared at Kyra. She couldn't even start to speak with her standing there, sniffling with that *Aren't-I-sweet-I-wouldn't-ever-do-anything-like-this* look on her baby face.

'Go and sort your room out, pet,' Mum said, quietly.

Pet! With her tiny ballerina body, Kyra looked about nine and acted younger. No wonder! She was never going to grow up, the way Mum and Dad treated her.

'See if there's anything else missing,' Mum added, 'before we decide whether to call the police.'

'Police!' Hannah said, as Kyra pushed past her and shimmied out.

No way could she have the police turning up, asking questions.

'Some of my jewellery's missing,' Mum said, sniffing loudly, 'and some other stuff. I've started a list.'

'But you can't call the police, you can't! I mean, what's the point? They won't do anything, will they? They'll just say it was my own fault.'

'Well, they'd be right about that,' said Dad, tipping rubbish into a cardboard box. 'And I don't suppose the house insurance covers gross bloody stupidity either, does it? We'll have to replace the carpets and half the bloody furniture. It's going to cost thousands, Hannah, thousands, do you understand?'

Hannah glanced round. Dad was exaggerating. It was bad but surely not that bad. Most of it would clean up, wouldn't it? Obviously her parents didn't think so because there were tears in Mum's eyes and Dad's face had reddened. The veins were standing out near his temples, where the hair was receding, like they always did when he got stressed.

'It just got out of hand,' she said. 'I didn't know what to do.'

'Phone us, call the cops or get one of the neighbours round?' Dad said.

Neighbours, was he kidding? They barely knew the neighbours, even though they'd lived here for most of her life. The houses were all detached, set back from the road at the end of long drives. Walled off, like private little prisons. So there'd been no one to notice the noise, the chaos.

'You could have phoned Jackie's parents or Clare's. Anyone, any adult, anyone with half a brain! Did you think of that?'

The answer was no. By the time all the real trouble kicked off, she was way past thinking straight. She still was. All the images were still grating in her head. One, the worst one, kept trying to push its way to the front. It was draining away what little energy she had, making her feel constantly sick, faint, confused and totally exhausted.

'I suppose you were too drunk to care,' said Dad. 'For goodness sake, you're only sixteen, Hannah. You're not even old enough to drink. I mean no one minds you having the odd glass but we're not just talking a glass or two, are we?' he added, looking down at the box, brimming with bottles and cans.

Hannah tried to look interested, contrite, even though she'd heard it all a million times before.

'God knows what you kids are doing to your livers,' he went on, 'not to mention any brain cells you might have left. I honestly don't understand you anymore, Hannah.'

Mum was tying up the top of the bin liner and staring at the mess that was left.

'It was him,' she suddenly said, 'wasn't it? This was Zak. He did this, didn't he?'

Hannah shook her head. How could Mum blame one person for all this? Not even Zak could cause so much damage on his own.

'He wasn't here,' Hannah said.

A pointless lie but she didn't want to talk about Zak. She didn't even want to think about him.

'Oh, come off it, Hannah,' said Mum, 'this has got Zak and his dodgy flaming mates stamped all over it. Your friends from school didn't wreck the place, did they?'

Hannah sank into one of the armchairs, which was wet and stinking of disinfectant. Mum had no idea. She only ever saw Hannah's friends from school when they were on their best behaviour. *Thanks for letting me stay. That spaghetti was lovely. Shall I help clear up?* She never saw Stacy swearing and chucking stuff at her mum. She never saw Jackie puking up when she'd been on the piss all night. She never saw the lads mouthing off and fighting each other. Mum's view of Hannah's school friends was stuck in a cosy little time warp, when they were all still relatively sweet and innocent like Kyra.

'I don't know what you're sitting down for,' Dad said, handing her a dustpan and brush. 'We haven't even touched the surface yet.'

As Hannah started to scoop up discarded cigarette ends that made her retch again. Mum stormed out while Dad launched into a full inventory of what was damaged and what was missing.

'I'll give you till tomorrow to get it all back,' he announced at the end of the list.

'How can I? I don't know who took it.'

The words came out sharper than she'd intended. She was trying to cooperate, trying to be reasonable, but it was hard when all she wanted to do was scream then go on screaming.

'Well somebody must know! Somebody must have noticed people walking off with stuff, so find out!'

'I don't think it could have happened during the party,' she said, hesitantly.

'Don't be stupid, Hannah, when the hell else could it have happened?'

He didn't bother waiting for an answer. He was off again, ranting about what needed to be done, how much it would all cost. Every word was thudding and rebounding in her head. It was hot, so very hot. She'd barely filled the dustpan and she was shattered already.

'Who broke the window?' Dad was asking.

'What window?'

'The kitchen window, you must have seen it, you must have noticed!'

She'd been in the kitchen. She'd stood right near the window when she was getting the glass of water but she hadn't noticed anything different.

'No, I didn't, I mean I don't know, I can't remember.'

'Well, what a surprise! You can't remember. It's because...'

Shut up, please just shut up. If he knew, if he knew what else had happened last night, but she could never tell him, never tell anyone. *Push it away, forget it, pretend it never happened* – but it wouldn't go. It was in her head, crawling all over her body, like a million squirming insects. She wanted to go for another shower but she couldn't just walk out.

'And the drugs, Hannah,' Dad was saying, his voice low and ominously quiet, 'who brought the drugs?'

'Drugs, what drugs?' she said.

This time, her words were coming out edgy, more panicky than she'd meant them to. It was like she was losing all control of her mind and her speech. Everything was happening too fast. All the questions, the accusations, were making her more and more dizzy, confused.

'Don't be stupid, Hannah,' Dad said. 'There's evidence all over the place. They didn't exactly clear up after themselves, did they?'

Dope, with any luck he was just talking about the dope – unless there was other stuff lying around. She hadn't bothered to check.

'I don't know,' she said. 'I didn't see any.'

'Oh sure,' said Dad, 'you didn't notice, just like you didn't notice the broken window or someone walking out with Kyra's new TV!'

'There were a few people smoking, OK. So what, everybody does.'

Dad's eyes widened. What was it with her parents? How could they be so bloody naïve? Hadn't they ever been young, didn't they read the papers or watch the news? Did they think they were living in some big protective suburban bubble, a drug-free zone?

'Everybody?' he said. 'You, Jackie, Clare?'

'No,' she said, backtracking before she dropped her friends in it big time, 'not us, but you know...'

'Zak,' said Mum, walking back into the sitting room, 'Zak and his bloody mates. I knew they'd been here, I knew you were lying. I've just phoned Jackie's mum. Jackie said Zak turned up.'

Oh, great thanks, Jackie.

'At about eleven o'clock.'

No, earlier, it was much earlier, not long after Shane, who'd turned up at exactly twenty past nine.

'With that Jed, Jackie said, and a dozen or so other lads.'

Bollocks, there were five or six that's all, including Zak and Jed, but Jackie was probably seeing double by that time!

'Just before all the trouble kicked off, according to Jackie,' Mum went on.

No, not all of it. Jackie was wrong again. There'd been mess before Zak's lot turned up; spilled drinks, discarded cans, cigarette ends all over the place. She'd tried to sort it, tried to clear up but no one cared, no one would help her. So at some point she'd just given up.

'Bit of a coincidence, don't you think?' Mum snapped. 'Jackie said they were all hyper.'

Yeah well, she was right about that, right about Zak at least. He'd bounded over to her, his eyes bright, the pupils huge. Unable to stand still, he was almost bouncing on the spot as he talked. The words came gushing out. Words she didn't want to hear.

'Aw, come on, Hannah.'

She'd felt his hands on her shoulders, moving down her arms, squeezing far too tight. He was hurting her, though probably not meaning to, until she'd pulled away.

'No, no way, Zak, I've told you, it's over, finished.'

'Why?'

'It just is, Zak!'

'Who are you looking at, anyway? Why d'yer keep looking over at Shane? What's bloody Shane got to do with anything?'

'Just go, Zak. I've got enough trouble.'

Shane had been talking to Eden, who was laughing, flirting like she did with all the lads. Then Shane had seen them looking at him and walked out of the room. She'd tried not to care. All that was over, Shane was with Lucy now and they showed no signs of breaking up. So she had to accept it, move on. She had moved on but in the wrong direction. She should never have got involved with Zak.

'I don't get it, Hannah. You and me, we're great together.'

Zak's hand creeping round the back of her neck, drawing her towards him again. Why was it so tempting? Why did he have to be so totally fit? Why not give it another chance, like he said? But no — he was trouble. He was too old for her. She hadn't thought so at first. He was only twenty, well nearly twenty-one now, but Mum had been right. He was too moody, too unpredictable and way too screwed-up.

He needed a bloody psychiatrist not a girlfriend. She couldn't handle him. They had nothing in common. He hung out with all the wrong people. That Jed guy for a start — he was totally deranged, seriously creepy. Eden had once had a bit of a fling with Jed but even she'd dumped him.

'No, don't touch me, stop it, Zak. I need to clear up. Look at it! Dad's gonna kill me.'

'I'll help you. Get everyone out, eh, just you and me?'

'No!'

'Please, Hannah, I've never felt like this about no one else.'

Why didn't he get it, what was so hard to understand? Were her eyes, her body giving off different messages to her mouth? Why was she so confused about how she felt?

'Jackie's really upset, her mum says.'

'What?' said Hannah, snapping back to the present.

'Poor Jackie,' Mum repeated, 'she's really upset.'

Poor Jackie? What had Jackie got to be upset about? What the hell had Jackie been saying?

41

'She's been really sick since she got home. She reckons somebody must have spiked her drink.'

Oh yeah, right, sure, and Jackie's mum believed that? Jackie hadn't just got pissed and lumbered herself with a massive hangover, as usual. Her drink had been spiked! Nice one, Jackie.

'And I can guess who was responsible,' Mum said.

'I bet you can!'

'Well it wouldn't take a genius to work it out, would it?' Mum snapped. 'I told you right from the start Zak was bad news.'

Zak. The name screamed in Hannah's head. Why did Mum have to keep saying it, why couldn't she just shut up, leave her alone? She was just making everything worse, if it could be any worse.

'I thought it was all over, anyway,' Dad pitched in. 'I thought you finished with Zak, or was that another lie?'

No, it wasn't a lie. She'd dumped him almost two weeks ago but he wouldn't leave her alone. He'd been phoning her, sending texts and e-mails, hanging around – positively bloody stalking her. Wearing her down until she'd almost...

'Oh, what's the point?' said Hannah, dropping the dustpan she'd been holding. 'Whatever I say, you won't believe me.'

Her legs, which had barely been supporting her, gave way completely and she crumpled to the floor.

'Hannah?' Mum said, rushing over, kneeling beside her. 'Are you all right?'

'Of course she's not all right,' Dad snarled. 'It's called a hangover.'

'Yes, well you'd know,' said Mum, suddenly redirecting her anger. 'You've had enough of them in your time. I told you we shouldn't have left her. I said she should have gone to Mother's with Kyra.'

'Don't,' said Hannah, 'don't start all that again.'

They'd gone on about it for weeks before they went away. Mum's first plan was to leave both her and Kyra at home together but no one had been overly keen on that idea.

'I'm not staying with Hannah,' Kyra had whinged, 'she bosses me all the time.'

'Yeah, like I want to baby-sit for a whole weekend,' Hannah had responded.

'I'm not sure it's fair on Hannah,' Dad had muttered.

What he'd meant, of course, was that he didn't trust her and Kyra together. He probably thought they'd have killed each other by the end of the weekend. And he might have been right!

'Anyway, I want to go to Gran's,' Kyra had announced.

Well she would! Gran spoiled her, like everybody did, and a couple of Kyra's pathetic little ballet-class friends lived near Gran.

'That's a better idea,' Mum had agreed, 'I'll be happier knowing you're both safe with Gran.'

'No way! I'm not going,' Hannah said.

She had nothing against Gran. Gran was always fine with her, even though Kyra was the favourite, but no way was she going to be farmed out there for a weekend. She was sixteen, for heaven's sake! Her parents were adamant, at first, but Dad eventually cracked.

He'd given way to her pleas that she was responsible, that she could manage on her own for a weekend and that she could cope. But she hadn't, had she? She'd screwed up big time. It was supposed to be a relaxing break for Mum and Dad, just the two of them, a chance to try and sort things out. They'd both been working so hard, getting stressed, rowing all the time about stupid, petty stuff. And now she'd just piled on more stress.

'I need to lie down, I need to go to bed,' she said.

'Maybe we should call a doctor,' said Mum,

helping her up. 'What if your drink was spiked, like Jackie's?'

'It wasn't,' said Hannah, her voice barely audible, 'no one was spiking drinks. Jackie was well pissed before the party started!'

'But this isn't like you, Hannah,' Mum said. 'I've never seen you this bad, not even when you'd been out with Zak till God knows what time.'

'Please,' Hannah groaned, 'lay off about him. It was a mistake, I know that, it's over, finished. Just let me go to bed.'

She stumbled out before either of them could try to stop her, went upstairs and lay down on the unmade bed. She closed her eyes, utterly exhausted. Her mind was drifting, half-awake, half-asleep.

She saw herself barging into the kitchen to get away from Zak, before she did something stupid. She remembered picking up a bottle, swigging from it. What was it, what was in it, what had she drunk? She didn't know. She couldn't remember the taste or the colour or the smell. The noise, she could remember the noise. All the people crowding into the kitchen — squashed together. There were too many people, too much noise. It was all getting completely out of control.

Looking for Stacy, Clare, Shane, Ravi, Mica, someone, anyone to help her, but they weren't around. She couldn't find them. Just crowds of people she hardly knew. Young, giggly girls who looked barely older than Kyra, older lads, a blur of faces and movement. And Jed, leaning against the sink, watching her. His eyes blue like hers but sort of hard and scary, his mouth twisted into a sneer.

Picking up another bottle and sitting down but she hadn't drunk anything that time. Or, at least she thought not. She'd stood up and walked round. That's right, she'd wandered outside and seen Jackie puking on the lawn. Then she'd turned, heading back to the kitchen, which had started to spin, making her clutch the side of the sink.

Arms round her waist. Thinking of him, of Shane, but it was Zak, bloody Zak again.

'Piss off, Zak.'

'You don't mean that.'

The arms tightening, her yelling at him, trying to push him away, knowing people were staring.

'I said piss off!'

Pushing him away, seeing him slip then hearing his head smack against — what? Not even caring, going upstairs, trying to get away. Pushing past snogging couples, wanting to lie down, sleep and escape from it all. Only it wasn't that simple. She'd opened her bedroom door and seen them! Shane and Eden, pulling apart. Shane shrugging then pushing past her, like she was no one, like she didn't matter!

Eden standing there smiling. Her face flushed, eyes bright, re-adjusting her skirt and top. Shane and bloody Eden — that was all she needed! Shane and Lucy, she'd just about accepted but now he was cheating on Lucy too.

A bell was ringing. Hannah reached for her phone but it wasn't her phone. It was the wrong sound completely. The doorbell, so probably someone for Mum and Dad, or at least she hoped it was. She really didn't want to see anyone. But then if it was one of her so-called friends, she didn't want them talking to Mum and Dad either. She sat up and swung her legs over the side of the bed. She was still wondering whether to go down, when the bedroom door opened and Clare walked in.

'What do you want?'

'I came to see how you are,' said Clare, walking over, sitting on the edge of the bed. 'I came to say sorry. God, you look terrible, look at your face!'

'You don't look too great yourself.'

Clare's auburn hair was scraped back, tied up in a ponytail, though it was barely long enough. Her face looked dry and blotchy, as if she'd been rubbing it. There'd be a lot of people who weren't exactly looking their best today.

'Yeah, that's what Kyra said,' Clare muttered.

'Kyra let you in?'

'Yeah, I came straight up. Well, as soon as Kyra would let me. She was moaning on about some stuff that was missing. God, she's a pain!'

'Tell me about it!'

'Anyway, I didn't much fancy bumping into your mum and dad, especially after I'd seen the state of the hall. I mean, it's even worse than I thought.'

'You could say that. They've cleaned up a lot of it.'

'Look, I'm sorry. I should have warned you what Jackie and Eden were doing but I really didn't think...'

No you didn't! Hannah wanted to scream. She wanted to tell Clare to go, leave her alone but maybe she shouldn't. Maybe she should let Clare stay. Maybe Clare could help her untangle things, work out the sequence of events, fill in the gaps.

'It's OK,' Hannah said. 'It wasn't your fault. I still don't really know what happened, how it got so bad.'

The words were catching in her throat, choking her.

'I don't know how...'

The words turned to sobs now, her eyes burning and her head pounding. Clare was hugging her, saying she was sorry over and over and mingled with Clare's voice was Eden's.

'It's not what you think. Hannah, wait. Don't tell no one. Don't tell Lucy, OK? It was nothing. We were talking, that's all. It's true! I mean, why the hell would I be interested in Shane? He's a kid! And anyway I've got a bloke, remember?'

'Oh right – yeah – Mystery Man!'

'Mystery Man, is that what you call him? OK, so I keep him away from you lot. But he's real, he's definitely real. It's serious,' she'd said, all sort of dreamy, not really like Eden at all, 'and I'm not, repeat not, interested in Shane.'

They'd looked pretty interested in each other. And Shane – well, she really didn't understand Shane any more. Once, not so long ago, Hannah had thought Shane would never cheat on anybody. But after the sleazy, sneaky way he'd got off with Lucy on that school trip then got bloody Jackie to eventually pass on the news!

It just so wasn't like Shane. He'd changed so much. Or had he always been that shallow and she just hadn't noticed before? And all the time she was thinking about Shane, she'd been looking at Eden who'd seemed happy to stare her out for a while before she eventually snapped.

'Oh for God's sake, Hannah, stop looking at me like that! Wait, listen! Me and Shane, we were just talking – we were talking about you!'

'Oh, sure.'

'We were! Shane – he's sort of upset, confused. He's not sure about Lucy anymore. He was asking about you and Zak, whether it was true you'd split up. That's why we came up here – to talk.'

'It didn't look like talking.'

'Oh grow up, Hannah, I gave him a hug, that's all. Hey, are you all right? You look like you're gonna throw up.'

'I'm fine. Leave me. Leave me alone.'

She remembered Eden leaving, the door closing, sinking onto the floor, which was spinning round and round then thinking she had to get up. Find Shane, talk to Shane, clear the mess and get everyone out. Was it true? Had Shane been asking about her? Was he still interested, was it possible, was Eden telling the truth? Or were those two – no – Shane, Eden, not possible, no way. Shane was with Lucy now — got mixed-up, everything was mixed up. Floor still spinning, eyes closing…

There was something white fluttering in front of her face. She took the tissue from Clare, wiped her eyes and tried to stop the sobs that were still bursting up from her chest.

'I went to my room. I think I blacked out,' she said.

She missed out the bit about Shane and Eden because she'd misunderstood, because it was just too complicated and it wasn't really what she needed to focus on.

'Is that when you got that bruise, d'yer reckon?'

'It might have been. Anyway when I woke up, it was quiet, everyone had gone.'

All but one.

'You don't know about the fight then?' Clare asked.

'Fight, no, I mean who?'

'I'm not sure who started it. I was outside with Mica.'

'You and Mica?'

'Yeah well, you know,' said Clare, 'that's parties for you! Anyway, we were in the back garden and suddenly something comes flying out through the kitchen window.'

'Ah, the window,' Hannah said, 'Dad was asking about that.'

'Then everyone's shouting and screaming. You know what it's like, someone kicks off and everyone joins in. God, you must have been well out, if you missed it! Mica said we should call the cops but then we heard someone yelling and the kitchen starts to empty. By the time we got inside, people were leaving. I looked round for you.'

Hannah nodded, the tears still pouring from her eyes though the sobs had stopped.

'We weren't as pissed as some. We were gonna stay. See if we could clear up.'

Yeah, sure, Clare.

'But he told us to go.'

'Who did?'

'Zak. It was Zak who got everyone out. I mean, you don't really argue with Zak, do you? Not in the sort of mood he was in!'

Maybe most people didn't but she had. When she'd stumbled downstairs, found him there on his own, lying on the settee, half-asleep, waiting for her. Waiting for her, starting up all over again, telling her he loved her.

'No, go away, get out!'

4

The narrow, covered alley at the back of the café was shady and quiet. Early on Monday afternoon, Zak leaned against the wall, letting the cold brickwork cool his back. He had a cigarette in one hand and his phone in the other, his thumb tapping in yet another message. When he'd finished, he checked again to see if she'd answered the half a dozen texts he'd sent the previous day. Or the two he'd sent earlier that morning. She hadn't.

'Zak, are you still out there?' his boss called from the kitchens.

When he'd finished the cigarette, Zak dropped it, grinding it onto the dry, dusty flagstones with his heel. He disturbed a small brown spider that had been lurking in a crack and watched as it scurried away by a cardboard box.

'Zak!' the boss called again.

Zak ignored him, wishing he could hide away as

easily as the spider. But he couldn't, so he sidled a bit further along the wall. He stared at his phone, willing it to ring, willing it to be Hannah. Even though he knew that there was no way, not now. He kicked his heel back against the wall, over and over, listening to the rhythmic thud. He knew it was his own fault for going to that party. He knew he should have just left it. He should have let it go, let Hannah go, like Jed kept saying.

'There's loads of other girls, mate,' Jed had said. 'It's not like you have trouble getting girls, is it? I mean what's so special about bloody Hannah?'

Zak stopped kicking for a moment. He knew Jed was right about him having no trouble getting girls and he was right about Hannah too.

'There's nothing special about Hannah!' Zak muttered. 'Get over it.'

He said, 'Get over it', twice more, but very quietly, in case the boss was still lurking. It didn't help though. He could say it as often as he liked but it didn't help. Sliding slowly down the wall he slumped onto the rough flagstones with his knees hunched up to his chest. He tried to make his mind totally blank but it didn't work. It was full of Hannah. It always was. It was like having some illness that you couldn't shake off.

Sometimes he wished he'd never met her. He'd managed to get through school without noticing her. But then that wasn't really surprising because she was only in Year Seven when he left, just before his exams in Year Eleven. And Zak wasn't noticing much then except his problems; his mum and her illness. He'd never even heard of Hannah until about three months ago when she'd turned up at the café one Saturday afternoon. With his eyes half-closed, Zak pictured her sitting at the table in the corner, on her own, flicking through some notes in a shiny blue folder, not really reading them.

'Hey,' a female voice said, making him jump.

Zak opened his eyes and looked up, half expecting, hoping to see Hannah, but it wasn't her. It was just Tasha standing there, her round, freckly face all hot and red. Her waitress's cap tilted over her left ear, about to slide right off her greasy, mousy hair.

'The boss says yer to come in now,' she said, ramming the cap into place. 'No one else can have their break till you get back.'

'Tell him I'm dead or something,' Zak said.

Tasha waddled off to report to the boss, her flat sandals flip-flapping on the flagstones. Zak knew he ought to get up, go back, but instead he opened his phone and found a picture of Hannah. She was smiling in a way she hadn't been that first day in the café. Her head had been down then, shoulders hunched, forehead screwed into a frown. She'd looked so pathetic he'd almost laughed when she said it was only boyfriend trouble! She'd hung around till he finished his shift then they'd gone for a walk and just talked for a bit. They did a lot of talking, him and Hannah. More than he'd done with any other girl.

'Zak! I don't care whether you're dead or not. Get your bloody arse back in here, now!'

Zak swore as he stood up and saw the boss standing on the back doorstep of the café. As soon as Zak started to move the boss dashed back inside so Zak carried on flipping through his pictures, as he ambled towards the door. The first one he'd ever taken of Hannah showed her sitting on a low wall in the park, mouth down-turned. She'd been whinging on about Shane, Lucy, school and how she couldn't concentrate on her revision. He'd taken the photo out of boredom when he'd got tired of listening.

'Mum and Dad'll kill me if I screw up,' she'd said, 'but I just feel – I don't know – I just miss him so much!'

Zak stopped walking as he moved onto another picture of Hannah and another. He had hundreds – like some pervy paparazzi stalker! There was Hannah in her garden, Hannah outside school with Clare and Jackie, Hannah in the café waiting for him to finish one of his shifts. He still wasn't sure how he'd got so involved with her. She wasn't even that pretty. Well, not compared to some girls he'd been with. But somehow she'd got to him. He'd ended up seeing her again and again – or at least when she could fit him in between revision and exams.

He snapped the phone shut, put it in his pocket and took out his lighter instead. Twirling it between his fingers, he flicked it on and off, watching the flame getting bigger, smaller and bigger again. He'd almost quit smoking when he was with Hannah. She didn't like it and it didn't bother him too much not to smoke when she was around. He stopped playing with the lighter, got a cigarette out and put it in his mouth but he didn't light it. He just held it there, thinking. There was something sort of natural about Hannah, some-thing that made him feel relaxed, less angry, more like he used to be. But then when the exams were over, just as it was getting really good, just as she'd started to loosen up a bit, she'd dumped him!

Zak swore, gave a final flick of the lighter then hurled it at the wall opposite. He heard it crack, watched bits of metal and plastic flying off it, scattering as it fell onto the flagstones. Stretching out his foot he stamped on what was left of the cheap, plastic lighter, listening to it cracking again. Then he pulled out another from his pocket and finally lit his cigarette.

'Don't bother,' the boss snarled, suddenly appearing right in front of him, as if he'd popped up out of a trapdoor. 'What the bloody hell's wrong with you today, Zak? Your break finished ten minutes ago and it's manic out there.'

'Yeah, right, tell me about it,' Zak said, taking a few quick drags on the cigarette.

'Listen, Zak,' said the boss. 'If there's anything wrong, if there's anything I can do—'

'There isn't!'

'It's not about Hannah, is it? I mean, I haven't seen her around for a while and—'

'No! It's nothin' to do with Hannah. That finished ages ago,' he said, shrugging. 'You know I don't do long-term shit.'

He hadn't exactly told the boss that they'd split. He hadn't gone out of his way to tell anybody, not least because he was still trying to work it out.

58

Hannah hadn't given any reasons for dumping him or at least not any that made sense. He'd tried everything to get her back except the one thing he couldn't do – turn into Shane! A picture of slimy, smarmy Shane flashed into his head and he knew that was it; that was the real problem.

It wasn't him Hannah wanted, it never had been. It was always bloody Shane. He rubbed the top of his forehead, as he reached the café door, feeling the bump where his head had smacked against the fridge-freezer, when Hannah had pushed him. He stubbed out his cigarette, shoved a mint in his mouth and glanced at his watch. It was only another two hours before his shift finished. By three o'clock he'd be free.

'Move it, Zak,' the boss said, hurrying inside.

'Yeah, all right,' Zak replied, kicking one of the bins, which rattled and echoed round the alleyway.

He'd barely got in the kitchen when the boss shoved two plates in his hand.

'Turkey salads, table twelve. And what've you done to your hand?' he added, glancing at Zak's knuckles, which he'd managed to keep hidden up until now. 'You been fighting again?'

'No,' Zak snapped.

He moved quickly before he did something stupid. Table twelve was outside, where most people were sitting today, crowded into the tiny area surrounded by the low barrier that marked off the edge of the café's territory from the rest of the square. Zak sighed and sucked hard on his mint so customers wouldn't complain about his breath.

They weren't usually this busy on a Monday but the sun had brought everyone out. He looked round at the shoppers in their stupid multi-coloured shorts and floppy hats, the office workers with their cotton shirts and sensible skirts or trousers. He sighed and started battling his way past whining babies in pushchairs, with the wheels sticking out from the tables getting in his way, and herds of little kids who were running round, shrieking. He resisted the temptation to trip one of the kids and smiled as he delivered the turkey salads.

No matter how bad he felt, Zak always managed to turn on a smile. He'd worked it out long ago.

'Pure economics,' he'd once told Hannah, 'the brighter the smile, the better the tips! I get enough most weeks to make up for the crap wage – well, almost.'

He'd had to add the last bit to explain why he was always borrowing off her and why the bank had refused him an overdraft.

'So where does it all go?' she'd asked.

'Car, I suppose,' he'd said. 'Insurance is mad. Then there's tax and petrol's not exactly cheap.'

He hadn't mentioned that drugs weren't exactly cheap either but she'd probably guessed that. She'd looked at him like his dad did sometimes just before he launched into one of his lectures.

Having off-loaded the salads, Zak looked around to see what else needed doing. A family was just getting up from table eight and, as he started to move across to clear the plates, he noticed a girl waving at him from behind the barrier. He screwed up his eyes against the glare of the sun, trying to see who it was and made out the small, slightly plump figure, the glint of auburn hair.

It was Hannah's friend, Clare, and she was definitely waving at him, which was a bit strange. The boss was watching from the café doorway so Zak started stacking the plates from table eight while Clare sidled round the barrier towards him.

'What d'yer want? I can't stay long,' he said, half turning his head towards the door where he guessed the boss was still lurking.

'Neither can I,' said Clare. 'I'm on my lunch break. I just wanted you to do something for me.'

'Uh?' he said, wondering why Clare would be asking for favours.

He didn't know Clare that well and she hardly ever used to speak to him when he was with Hannah.

'Well, it's for Hannah really.'

'Hannah! You've seen her then, since the party?'

'Yesterday,' Clare said, 'but Hannah doesn't know I'm asking,' she added, talking fast, rattling out her request.

'Oh, that,' said Zak, 'yeah, I already know about that.'

'How, who told you?'

'I heard a few rumours yesterday.'

'Blimey, that got round quick.'

'Yeah, well, you can't keep nothing quiet round here. So no probs, I'm already onto it. Saw a few people last night so it might all be sorted by later this afternoon.'

He knew it wouldn't make any difference to the way Hannah felt but then it was the least he could do.

'Hey,' he said as Clare started to walk away, 'give me your number and I'll let you know, OK?'

He didn't particularly want to let Clare know how it went but he'd decided it might be handy to have Clare's number, a line of contact with Hannah. Clare could be useful.

5

Hannah lay on her unmade bed, where she'd been lying since late on Sunday afternoon – so more than twenty-four hours now. The hangover had all but gone and with it the numbing effect of the alcohol, leaving a different sort of sickness, a different kind of pain. She couldn't really analyse it. It was like a dull ache, a tiredness that she couldn't shake off. She didn't want to move, do anything, or talk to anyone. She vaguely remembered talking to Clare but couldn't remember her leaving. There was just a half-memory of Clare saying she'd ask around, see if she could find out who'd been nicking stuff.

Clare was OK really. They'd been best mates in primary school and through to Year Seven. Then, sometime around Year Eight, allegiances had changed. Clare had joined Jackie's crowd. Hannah still wasn't quite sure why, except that everyone who was anyone was hovering round Jackie by then.

Well apart from her and Lucy, of course. They'd hung back on the fringes, still being good girls. And that's the way it had stayed until recently when Lucy hadn't left her much choice. It was hang around with Jackie, Stacy and Clare or have no decent mates at school at all.

Rolling onto her side, Hannah tried to forget about shifting friendships and focus on what had happened after Clare had left yesterday. At some point in the evening Mum had wandered in and asked if she wanted anything to eat. As if! Drifting off to sleep again, waking occasionally to drink the water someone had left on her bedside table then staggering to the loo to throw up yet again. This morning, she hadn't been able to face going to work.

'You've only been there two weeks,' Dad had needlessly pointed out. 'And you're already off sick. Hardly a good start, is it?'

Mum had taken the day off work too but that was different.

'Your mum's got to make phone calls, wait in for people to measure carpets and mend windows, thanks to you,' Dad had snapped.

The window man had eventually arrived about half-past three. He'd been banging and thudding ever since, setting off Hannah's headache, making her reach for the paracetamol again. How many had she taken? Did it matter, did she care? With any luck they'd send her back to sleep and she'd never wake up.

Clare had sent a text around lunch time saying that Jackie and Liam had called in sick too and that the manager had been asking questions. Well he would. It was one of the problems of loads of them working in the same place but it was the obvious choice. Quite close by, easy to get to. They were always desperate for holiday staff to push the trolleys, stack the shelves and man the checkouts. Yeah, boring, but she'd been looking forward to working there, earning a bit of money. Now, she was finding it hard to look forward at all, to focus on anything except what had happened.

There'd been texts from other people but she hadn't bothered to read many of them. She hadn't answered the calls either. She shifted again, curling up, wrapping her arms round her stomach, which felt sore and empty. She hadn't eaten anything since Saturday, nothing at all. She'd have to try to eat something soon but the mere thought made her feel sick.

Thud, thud, thud. Was the window man ever going to stop? Just how long could it take to fix a bloody window? He'd been at it for over two hours. Another *thud*, a different kind of *thud*, and the bedroom door burst open.

'Are you still in bed?' Kyra asked.

'Looks that way.'

'While the rest of us do all the work, nice one, Hannah, you're such a lazy pig!'

She spat the last word as if 'pig' was a really daring insult.

'Mum's completely knackered,' Kyra added, her voice a high-pitched whine like a dentist's drill, 'and there's loads still to do. I've just been putting some rubbish out the front.'

'Good for you.'

'And there's someone waiting for you,' Kyra said, edging closer to the bed.

'What?'

'Someone out the front, waiting for you,' said Kyra, speaking slowly like she was talking to a complete idiot.

'Who?'

'Can't you guess?'

'No,' said Hannah, lunging forward, grabbing Kyra's wrist with both hands and twisting it until tears formed in Kyra's eyes. 'I can't so you better tell me.'

'Zak,' said Kyra, pulling away. 'He's sitting in his stupid car, at the bottom of the drive. So you better get rid of him or I'm telling Mum.'

Zak, oh shit!

6

Shane changed out of his paint-splattered overalls, had a quick shower, got dressed and darted down-stairs. He pushed open the lounge door but didn't go in.

'Right, see yer later,' he called to his mum.

'You off out?' Mum said, looking up from her laptop. 'What about your dinner?'

'Not hungry, haven't got time,' Shane said. 'Blame Dad! We were supposed to finish by six but there was a problem with a door. So we didn't leave till quarter-past. Then Dad made us stop off on the way home.'

'At the pub by any chance?' Mum asked.

'I wish! No he was doin' an estimate for paint-ing some woman's lounge.'

'As if he didn't have enough work on already!' Mum said.

'Yeah, exactly,' Shane said, hurrying into the

hall, before Mum could launch into full manic fuss mode about him missing dinner.

'Are you sure you don't want dinner first?' she called after him. 'It's nearly ready. It's tuna-pasta bake.'

Tuna-pasta bake, his favourite. He stopped by the door. But no! Lucy had invited him round on a Monday night, when her Mum was at work. Not the sort of chance he wanted to miss, especially with things as they were.

'No, it's all right,' he said, bending down to put his trainers on, trying to ignore the smell drifting through from the kitchen.

His stomach rumbled as he stood up. He'd only had a sandwich, a packet of crisps, an apple and a Kit Kat for lunch and, even then, they hadn't actually stopped work! Working with Dad in the holidays was all right. He enjoyed it – most of the time. But there was no contract, no rules, no set hours and not even the minimum bloody wage!

He went out, slamming the door behind him. Lucy was more important than tuna-pasta bake and at least she'd made the first move. She'd seemed OK when she'd phoned earlier. She hadn't mentioned Hannah or Eden or the party or nothing. But then you could never really tell with

Lucy, especially these days. Her mood could have changed again by now.

When he got to the front gate he glanced at his watch then set off jogging. There was no need to text her. She'd said half-past seven and he could easily be there before eight if he kept up this speed. Trouble was he couldn't! He was slowing down before he'd even got to the end of the road. It was so bloody hot! He paused to get his breath and wipe the sweat off his face. His jeans were sticking to his legs and the air felt all heavy and clammy, like there was a storm on its way.

He set off again, jogging more slowly, only picking up speed when he got near the flats. He checked the time as he stumbled into Lucy's block. 8:05 – so not too bad. Then he saw the sign on the lift.

OUT OF ORDER

Oh, great! Three flights of stairs. By the time he got to Lucy's door, he was breathing heavily and his heart was racing like he needed a pacemaker. *Oh God, he was so unfit these days! Maybe his mum was right. Maybe he should start training again. Dump Lucy, forget about girls and concentrate on sport, like Anil. At least sport was straightforward, simple. Girls were too complicated. Lucy, Eden, Hannah –* no, he really didn't want to think about all that.

Instead, he just waited, mind blank, letting his breathing steady before ringing the bell. He took a quick sniff at his armpits, hoping he didn't smell too sweaty. Girls could be funny about stuff like that, especially Lucy. OK, not too bad. He'd smelled worse! He ran his fingers through his hair and fixed a smile on his face. Sorted!

The door opened. His smile disappeared.

'Eden!'

He tried not to look fazed but he couldn't help it. What the hell was going on? Eden didn't usually hang out with Lucy. She didn't exactly hang around with any of their crowd, not even Jackie very much. Hannah's party had been an exception.

'Hi, Shane,' she said, winking at him, 'did you get my texts?'

'Er, yeah.'

'You just didn't bother to answer them.'

'I was going to,' he mumbled.

But he wasn't cos he had no idea what to say. Eden had been a mistake – mistake number one, on Saturday night. Eden was only playing with him. He'd known that all along – he wasn't stupid! But she was nineteen and totally, totally fit. He was hardly gonna refuse, was he?

'It's OK,' she said, 'I was just being – friendly.'

'Yeah, I know. I mean, I didn't expect . . . I knew it was only . . .'

He gave up because Eden wasn't listening. She was leading the way through the narrow hall to the lounge. She turned and smiled at him as they reached the door. Shane peered past her. Oh bugger – not a cosy night with Lucy then, or even a less-than-cosy threesome!

There weren't that many people but it was enough to make the tiny room look crowded, enough to totally ruin his night! Clare and Mica were sitting close on the settee, meaning the rumours were probably true. Ravi and Liam were sprawled on the floor, still looking wasted but not quite as wasted as Stacy who was slumped, asleep with her mouth drooped open.

Eden flopped into an armchair. Lucy was in the other. She didn't bother to get up or even look at him. There were bottles of Coke, lemonade and sparkling water set out on the small table. Great, a soft-drinks-only night and Lucy in one of her moods. He may as well go home. Would there be any tuna-pasta bake left?

'Aren't you going to sit down?' said Eden, patting the arm of her chair.

She smiled again. Her lips were all shiny with pale-pink gloss. Her green eyes were sly, cat-like, edged in black liner. Then she slowly crossed her long, fake-tanned legs. Bloody hell! Shane wiped his forehead. He saw Ravi and Liam positively slavering.

Dream on! Eden was well out of their league. Clare and Stacy were both quite pretty, Lucy was hot and Hannah he didn't even want to think about. But Eden – Eden was something else again and she knew it. He was amazed she'd even looked at him let alone – God, she was such a bitch!

This get-together was her idea. It had to be. She was up to something. Like she hadn't caused enough bloody trouble already! Shane shifted from foot to foot, wondering whether to sit down. Luckily everyone had started talking again, as if they didn't much care whether he stayed or went.

A thought flashed through his mind that Eden had set him up right from the start. It was some sort of test. A trap he'd fallen straight into. Her and Lucy could be in it together or, even worse, her and Hannah. Girls were like that. They were devious; they stuck together.

Except Eden wasn't quite the girly-pack type. She was more of a lone hunter, like a cheetah. Yeah, that was Eden, a cheetah – all long legs and sharp claws. She caught him staring at her again, so he turned his head away. OK, stop being paranoid. Maybe Eden was here because she was bored, pissed off like she'd been on Saturday. Mystery Man had probably told her he was working again – whoever he was. Nobody knew, of course, cos Eden wasn't saying.

'Must be someone from college,' people had said, at first.

But that didn't make much sense. There'd be no need to be secretive about a guy from college. Unless it was an older guy, a married guy, one of the lecturers or something, like Jackie reckoned.

'That'd explain all the secrecy, the times he can't get to see her,' Jackie had said. 'You know she even dresses different when she's off to see him, more sort of sophisticated, more grown-up, have you noticed?'

Nobody had, so they had to take Jackie's word for it. Not that Shane cared who the guy was or what Eden wore when she was with him. He just hoped Mystery Man would text Eden soon. Arrange to meet up, keep her occupied and get her out of the bloody way! He realised his head had swivelled round and he was looking at her again. By the look of her micro-skirt, it didn't seem like

Eden was expecting a call from Mystery Man any time soon. Not exactly sophisticated!

'You staying, Shane, or what?' Eden said.

Lucy had her head down so her hair was flopping round her face but he knew she was scowling. Shane could feel lines of sweat dripping from his forehead.

'Can I open a window? It's too hot.'

'They're open,' Lucy said.

'Oh, yeah, right,' he said, edging over to the table.

He poured himself a Coke. He swigged it back, almost choking as the bubbles fizzed in his dry throat and made their way up into his nose. He ignored Eden's unspoken invitation to sit by her and perched instead on a small stool next to Lucy. She still wouldn't look at him.

'You missed one hell of a party on Saturday,' Eden told Lucy.

'So I hear.'

'It's not funny,' Clare said, as Liam started to snigger. 'Hannah's parents are going ballistic and she's in a right state.'

'How do you know?' said Eden. 'No one's been able to get in touch. She's not answering her phone. Jackie's tried, in between puking, and I've tried,' she added, pointedly.

Shane could see people trying not to look too surprised. Caring about people, phoning about their state of health, wasn't really Eden's thing. And she was no great fan of Hannah's.

'I went round yesterday,' Clare said.

'Oh,' said Eden, 'so how was she?'

'Not good,' said Clare, shaking her head slightly, 'it was like...'

'What?' said Eden.

'I dunno,' said Clare, 'she was just crying all the time, like there was something else going on, something more than the hangover and coping with her parents and stuff. Something she was holding back, something she wasn't saying.'

Eden's eyes flicked from Clare to Shane and back again. Shane could feel his throat tightening. *Change the subject. Talk about something, anything, else.* But he couldn't. He couldn't think of anything to say.

'Probably just the fallout from her parents,' Liam said. 'I mean, they're pretty uptight at the best of times and, like, the house was a total mess.'

'Anyone know who broke that window? Who started the fight?' Mica asked.

Thanks, Mica, fights were good. Fights were safe.

'No use looking at me,' Shane managed to say. 'I

wasn't even there by then. I left early,' he added, risking a glance at Lucy.

It was straight after Hannah had burst in on him and Eden, but he couldn't tell Lucy that!

'It was a couple of Zak's mates,' said Liam, 'over some money or something. That Jed bloke started it, I think, with that blond spotty one.'

Zak's mates – Zak . . . Hannah – not so safe.

'Now why aren't I surprised?' Eden drawled. 'What a bunch of losers. I don't know why Hannah went out with him in the first place.'

Eden was smiling across at him again. She knew exactly why! And she seemed to have conveniently forgotten that she'd once been out with Jed, the biggest loser of the lot. Or maybe she really had forgotten. From what Jackie said, Eden had been out with loads of lads and didn't exactly keep count.

'I mean talk about desperate,' Eden said, 'a real rebound job.'

'Zak's not that bad,' said Clare. 'He's OK when he's not with his mates – I mean, at least he got everyone out in the end.'

'Yeah and he's been trying to get some of the missing stuff back,' said Liam.

Shane frowned. This was the first he'd heard about anything going missing.

'He came round to mine last night,' Liam was saying, 'scared the shit out of me.'

Some admission – there weren't many people Liam was scared of.

'Why you?' said Ravi. 'You didn't nick nothing, did you?'

'No! But Zak reckoned somebody did. You know Zak. There's not much he doesn't get to know about one way or another. Anyway some asshole gave him the name Liam and he thought they meant me!'

'What other Liam could they mean?' Mica said, 'we don't know no other Liams, do we?'

'Anyway, what did Zak do?' Ravi asked.

'Nothing much. In the end he believed me, thank God! He reckoned they might have meant Lee, not Liam.'

'Lee Broadhurst?'

'Probably, anyway Zak went off muttering about what he'd do to him when he found him.'

'What a hero,' said Eden. 'With any luck he'll beat Lee Broadhurst to a pulp and get himself arrested.'

'At least he's doing something,' said Clare, 'and it's not even like the party was his fault or anything, is it?'

'You sayin' it were my fault?' Eden snapped.

'No,' Clare muttered.

'Good,' said Eden. 'Anyway, what's with you, defending Zak all of a sudden? Don't tell me you fancy him!' she added, with a shriek. 'You're not after one of Hannah's cast-offs?'

Eden glanced at Lucy as she spoke. Mica shuffled even closer to Clare, putting his arm round her.

'Ooops, sorry,' said Eden, laughing, although it wasn't clear who she was apologising to, or even if she was really apologising at all.

The room suddenly darkened and a heavy burst of thunder made Lucy shriek and woke Stacy up. Shane looked at his watch. He'd only been there twenty minutes but it felt like hours. He wanted to make some excuse and just go. But if he did, if Eden hung around, waiting until her and Lucy were on their own, things might get tricky.

No, it was best to wait, stick it out. Eden was playing with him. She was mucking around, passing time till she could see Mystery Man again. Her texts didn't mean anything. She probably wouldn't say anything to Lucy – but it was best not to give her the chance. Anyway if he hung around long enough, till the others had gone, till him and Luce were on their own – well, who knew what might happen. His luck could still be in.

7

Mum strode into the lounge early on Tuesday morning, pulled back the curtains, turned, looked at Hannah lying on the sofa and screamed.

'God, you gave me a shock,' she said. 'What on earth are you doing in here? Have you been down here all night?'

Hannah didn't answer because she wasn't really sure how long she'd been there. The storm had kept her awake. It had built up slowly, the thunder rumbling for what seemed like hours before thick drops of rain had started pelting her bedroom windows. At some point, in the early hours, she'd wandered downstairs in a sort of daze. She remembered standing by the front window for ages watching forks of lightning and sheets of rain beating against the glass.

Then she'd flicked through the messages on her phone, deleting them all. Most of them were from

Zak, asking how she was! Fortunately her parents hadn't seen him lurking outside, yesterday. In fact, nobody had seen him except Kyra. When she'd eventually dragged herself off the bed and gone to look, there was no sign of him. She wondered if it was just Kyra's pathetic idea of a joke – like it was funny, like any of it was funny.

There'd been texts from other people too, dozens of them, not so different from Zak's, asking how she was. She couldn't answer them because she barely knew herself. There was such a rush of feelings that they'd all somehow collided and blurred into a grey nothingness. It was as though she couldn't feel anything at all, as though her body, her mind had totally shut down. As though it was a shadow Hannah, standing there by the window, watching the rain.

Finally she'd closed the curtains and dropped, exhausted, onto the sofa. When she'd woken up, the worst of the storm had passed. It was still raining; lighter now but persistent, like it was never going to stop. Her back ached as she stretched her legs, uncurling, trying to sit up.

'You'd better shower and get dressed,' Mum was saying. 'What time's your shift?'

Oh, God, work. She just couldn't face it; not today, not tomorrow, not ever.

'Ten o'clock, I think,' she said. 'Yeah, I do ten till four on Tuesdays. But I'm not going in. I'll give them a ring in a bit.'

One day at a time, just cope with one day at a time. She'd get over it eventually, she had to.

'No you won't,' Mum said. 'You're not having any more time off. You can go in.'

'I can't.'

'Rubbish,' Mum snapped. 'How long can it take to get over a hangover?'

A hangover, if only that's all it was! She could feel a pain tightening across her ribs, the pressure building behind her eyes, like something inside her was going to explode. She had to get a grip, get some sort of control. She had to stop bloody thinking about it!

'Come on, Hannah,' Mum said. 'Get yourself moving. I haven't got time to argue. I've got to take Kyra to Gran's then get to work myself.'

As if responding to the sound of her name, Kyra appeared, followed by Dad with his jacket and tie in his hand.

'Ugh, it still stinks in here,' said Kyra.

'Don't I know it,' said Mum.

'Right I'm off,' Dad said, putting his jacket on and draping his tie round his neck.

Just another few minutes and they'd all be gone. There'd been no more talk of getting the police involved but maybe her parents had already reported the missing stuff, gone behind her back. She didn't really care what they'd done as long as she didn't have to answer any more questions, as long as people left her alone. Kyra gave Dad a hug, he kissed the top of her head and walked out, barely looking at Hannah.

'I mean it, Hannah,' Mum said. 'I'll be going in ten minutes and I want to see you showered and dressed by then.'

'What are you staring at, freak?' Hannah hissed at Kyra, as soon as Mum walked out.

Before Kyra could answer, the doorbell rang.

'It'll be Dad,' Kyra said, as she darted out. 'I bet he's forgotten something again.'

She was right. It was Dad, but he hadn't forgotten anything. He appeared in the lounge, carrying a large cardboard box.

'I found this in the garage,' he said, easing it onto the floor.

It was obvious what was inside. The flaps of the box were open and Hannah could clearly see Kyra's missing television. Kyra gave one of her silly little shrieks, dropped to her knees and started rummaging about, pulling out DVDs, games and one of Mum's jewellery boxes. It wasn't hard to work out where the stuff had come from. It had to be Zak! That's why he'd been lurking yesterday. He hadn't nicked the stuff, she felt sure, but he'd known where to look, who to scare and how.

'Looks like someone's had an attack of conscience,' said Dad.

Conscience – yeah right – like Zak ever did conscience.

'My Nintendo's still missing!' Kyra was whining, as Mum came back in. 'The games are there but the machine's not.'

'Most of it's back though.' Mum bent down and picked out another small jewellery box.

'And there's a bin liner full of stuff still in the garage,' said Dad. 'I'll go and get it.'

'Hannah will you get up off there!' Mum shouted, rubbing her back as she straightened up.

Hannah obeyed. If she wanted to avoid a full-blown row, she'd have to go through the motions, have a shower and pretend she was going to work.

'What about my Nintendo?' Kyra wailed, before either Dad or Hannah could take so much as a step.

'Will you shut up about your bloody Nintendo! It's probably in the bin bag!'

Hannah bit her bottom lip. She shouldn't have said that. She should have kept her mouth shut, walked out and left them to it.

'Hannah!' Dad yelled, as Kyra predictably burst into tears.

'What? It's only a bloody machine and if it's not there I'll buy her a new one!'

Why wasn't her mouth listening to her brain? Why weren't her legs working? Why didn't she just walk out?

'With what?' Mum said. 'You won't have any money if you don't get yourself back to work.'

Suddenly they were all talking at once, filling the room with their voices: Kyra whining, Dad shouting, Mum moaning.

'You're going to work, Hannah.'

'And you'll be paying for more than the Nintendo! There's still the suite to replace.'

'And my door to mend.'

On and on and on and on. The list, the inventory of damage, the instructions, the orders and blame, all crashing onto her aching head, like any of it was important, like any of it mattered!

'Shut up! Shut up about your...'

'Hannah!' Dad yelled, as a string of words she never used at home burst out of her mouth.

'Is that all you care about, your bloody carpets and your coffee table? What about me?'

The words were spilling out. She had to stop.

'You?' Dad said. 'Oh – so you're suddenly the victim in all this? We're supposed to feel sorry for you, are we?'

The sharpness in his voice was like a spear piercing through her empty, aching gut. The pain was overriding her senses, forcing out the words she wanted to hold back, words that just gushed out, like the bloody rain crashing through the guttering.

'You don't understand – something happened – at the party.'

'I can see that!' Dad snapped.

'No, not just to the house – after the party – something happened. I can't stop thinking about it, it's driving me insane. He wouldn't listen, he wouldn't go away.'

The words were fading, almost whispered, but they wouldn't stop. Why was she doing this? She bit down harder on her lip but still the words came, forcing her mouth to open, forcing themselves out.

'He wouldn't listen – he wouldn't stop – I didn't want to – I told him to stop.'

'Hannah,' Mum said, her face already pale, her eyes hazy, 'what are you saying?'

86

'You know – you know what I mean.'

Mum, Dad and Kyra were all staring at her, the whimpered, whispered words somehow still hanging there, in the silence. She didn't need to spell it out. They knew. Even Kyra understood. What had she done?

'Hannah,' Mum said, quietly, as Kyra started to cry again, 'oh, Hannah, no.'

'Who?' said Dad, his fists clenching. 'Tell me who it was!'

She couldn't, she couldn't bear it. She turned away from them. She didn't want them near her. As Mum moved towards her, Hannah darted out, ran upstairs into the bathroom and locked the door. She stood with her back against it and let herself slide down. Her legs were outstretched, her eyes fixed on the rim of the bath, gleaming white. The whole bathroom was clean, fresh, smelling faintly of lemon. Someone had been busy in here, sometime while she'd been sleeping. She still wanted to sleep. Her eyelids were pressing down and closing.

'Come on, Hannah, let's get you upstairs, before you pass out again. Come on, it's OK. I'll look after you. Careful, watch the stairs! Come on, nearly there.

Lie down. I'll stay with you, OK, just while you fall asleep. It's all right.'

She was so tired, so very tired. His hand was stroking her hair, the other hand sliding across her body, down her leg.

'No!'

'Hannah, open the door, love,' Mum was pleading, 'let me in. Hannah, answer me!'

'Go away.'

'Please, Hannah, open the door.'

Pressing her hands down hard on the floor, she pushed herself up. She'd have to do it. She'd have to face them sometime. As soon as she'd pulled the catch, almost before the door was fully open, Mum was there. Mum's arms were wrapped around her, holding her tight, steering her out into the hall, towards Mum's bedroom. Hannah felt herself sinking onto the bed, onto the softness of the duvet.

'Tell me,' Mum urged. 'Tell me what happened.'

Hannah shook her head. She could feel Mum next to her, shivering, barely holding back tears.

'No. I can't. I shouldn't have – it was my own fault. I shouldn't have let him near me – I was so drunk.'

'No!' said Mum. 'It wasn't your fault. Ssshhh, it's OK, it's OK.'

Both of them starting to cry, crying in a time that felt like for ever. Then Mum's voice again, low and hoarse.

'Your dad's taken Kyra to Gran's. We thought it best. He'll be back soon.'

'He won't tell her? He won't tell Gran? Don't tell anyone.'

'You have to, Hannah. You have to report this. Your dad's already phoned the police.'

'No! I can't tell them, you don't understand. I shouldn't have told you. I never meant to. I don't want anyone to know! Forget it. Just forget I ever said it.'

8

Zak turned the key in the lock and pushed open the door. He did it quietly even though he knew there wouldn't be anyone in. His dad would be at work by now but sneaking in and out had become a bit of a habit. He headed straight upstairs to shave, shower and change his clothes, which were damp with sweat. He threw his jacket down on the bed, which had been neatly made up since he was last here. His clothes had been put away too.

He wished his dad wouldn't do that, that he'd just leave things alone. Zak opened the wardrobe and pulled out a black T-shirt. It had been washed, ironed and carefully folded. He wanted to scrunch it up, pull all the others out of the wardrobe, throw them on the floor and stamp on them. It would be stupid and childish, he knew, but it drove him nuts the way Dad insisted on doing everything just right: the shopping, cooking, ironing and cleaning.

It was like he was trying to prove he could be Dad and Mum all rolled into one. Like he was trying to take her place, as if anyone could!

'Hey.'

Zak swung round at the sound of his dad's voice.

'What you doing here?' Zak asked.

'I live here, remember?' said Dad, standing there in his old-man dark trousers and faded green polo shirt.

'I thought you'd be at work,' Zak said.

'I've taken a week's holiday. I need to get the garden sorted but it's just started to rain again so I came in.'

The word garden scraped in Zak's head because gardening was something else his mum used to do. She had a sort of knack with plants in a way that his dad just didn't.

'It's a mess,' Dad added. 'Hopefully this is only a shower because I really need to get on with it. Honestly, the flaming weather changes by the minute! So what are you doing today?'

'I'm in work at eleven. I need to go soon,' he added, before Dad could suggest they spent a cosy morning weeding and lawn mowing together!

'I thought Tuesdays were your day off.'

'It is usually, but we're busy, the boss wants me in.'

Zak had said it firmly, confidently, but it was only half true. The café was busy. He'd been doing extra shifts, but the boss didn't need him today so Zak had made other plans. He was thinking about them now as he looked at his dad, knowing they were stupid plans, pointless plans but he'd do them anyway because he wouldn't be able to stop himself.

'I've hardly seen you,' Dad said. 'You haven't been home for a while.'

All the words were clipped, short, like the two of them were strangers, which in a way Zak had to admit they were.

'I've popped back once or twice but you weren't in. I've been staying at Jed's.'

That wasn't true either. Jed's hostel had clamped down on overnight squatters so Zak had been dossing in the park most nights, while the weather had been fine. He'd sleep almost anywhere, do anything, to avoid coming back while his dad was around.

'You haven't been answering your phone.'

'Yeah well, I've been busy,' Zak said, knowing how feeble it sounded.

'Look, I'm sorry about the other week,' said Dad, sitting down on the edge of the bed. 'I shouldn't have said all that stuff...'

Zak waited as his dad paused. He knew there was always a 'but' and sure enough it came.

'But you've got to get yourself sorted, Zak.'

'So you keep saying.'

'I miss her too,' said Dad, glancing at the small framed photo of Mum on the windowsill. The photograph that had been taken at Christmas, just six months before she died, the only one Zak had in his room.

Zak felt his legs go so weak he had to lean against the wardrobe. He hated talking about it. He hated Dad mentioning her. Even after almost five years, Zak could barely believe his mum wasn't coming back. He looked down at the floor so Dad couldn't see his eyes.

It had all happened so quickly. His mum had been fine over Christmas and into the New Year. She'd gone to work, done all the things she usually did, managing to pack about thirty hours into a day. Then one day, in early February, she'd complained of stomach and back pains. She hadn't bothered too much at first so Zak and his dad hadn't either.

She'd said it was a winter bug or something she'd eaten but the pains got worse and started to spread. They'd eventually persuaded her to see a doctor who'd sent her for some tests but it was all too late. She was only forty-one. Zak heard a steady banging and realised he was rocking against the wardrobe and that his dad was staring at him.

'What?' Zak said. 'Well, you don't expect your mum to just die like that, do you? You think she's always gonna be there telling you to do your homework, have a shower and eat your bloody greens.'

An image of Mum peeling mountains of sprouts for Christmas dinner popped into Zak's head. It was one of the things that always freaked him – remembering how keen Mum had been on healthy food. She didn't smoke either and only ever had the odd glass of wine but none of it helped. She died anyway when some alkies and drug addicts lived well into their seventies and beyond. It was the unfairness that got to him, the total bloody random unfairness.

'Anyway,' Zak snapped, 'it's got nothing to do with that. It's got nothing to do with Mum. I'm over all that. I'm fine. There's nothing wrong with me. It's you, making a big deal out of everything. "Why don't you go to college, Zak? Get your qualifications, Zak," like any of it matters any more!'

He could feel his shoulders tightening, his fists clenching, his head sizzling, burning, as if there were great bundles of fireworks in there trying to blast their way out.

'What's happened to your hand?' Dad asked, ignoring Zak's rant.

'Oh, don't you frickin' start. The boss has already had a go! I haven't been fighting, right?'

It wasn't exactly true. He'd had to come on a bit heavy to get the last few bits of Hannah's stuff back but that wasn't how he'd grazed his knuckles. His dad's forehead had creased. Zak knew what was next. He knew exactly what his dad was going to say because it was something he'd been saying for the past four years in between the pleas for Zak to do his exams and pick up where he'd left off. His dad seemed to think you could go on like before, pretending it hadn't happened, pretending Mum was still around.

'No, no way,' Zak answered before the question was even formed, 'I'm not going to counselling and I don't need anger management.'

He brushed away a niggling doubt that maybe he did. After Saturday night, after what had happened at Hannah's – he wasn't exactly proud of that.

'Look, I haven't been fighting, OK. I can cope, I can handle it.'

His dad sighed, summing up four years of rows, four years of the arguments that went round and round in circles, getting nowhere.

'But you can't,' Dad said, 'you've never really come to terms with it.'

'Mum got ill, she died. These things happen, what's there to come to terms with?'

'Listen to yourself, Zak,' Dad said. 'You need some help before you get yourself into serious trouble.'

'I'm not gonna get in any trouble, right? Look, I've gotta have a shower and go. I'm late.'

'Will you be back tonight?'

Zak glanced outside. The rain had stopped again but he couldn't rely on it staying dry. The park was no good in the rain and he'd run out of options. Last night, during the storm, he'd slept in the car but it wasn't exactly comfortable and he couldn't do that for ever. Not least because the police sometimes came sniffing round and Zak tried to avoid them as much as possible.

'Yeah, probably,' he mumbled.

As he walked out of the bedroom he could feel eyes following him but he knew it wasn't Dad. It was Mum. She was watching him, she was always watching him and she didn't much like what she saw.

9

Keeping her head down, Hannah focussed on the bottom of her jeans, the crisscross pattern of straps on her sandals and the bright varnish on her toes. She knew they were all watching her, waiting expectantly, but she didn't look up. If she kept looking at her feet, maybe the cops would just go away. She hadn't asked for any of this. She didn't want it. It had all been Dad's idea.

He'd got back from Gran's about ten o'clock and sometime after that the two police officers had arrived. Mum had helped her to get dressed and taken her downstairs. She hadn't wanted to go but she was too tired to argue and they couldn't make her say anything, could they, not if she didn't want to? Mum had asked her over and over about what had happened, who was involved, but she'd just kept shaking her head.

'We can't really help,' the policeman was saying,

as though he had a million better things to do, 'if she doesn't want to talk to us.'

'Hannah,' Mum pleaded, 'you have to tell them.'

'Maybe she's not sure,' the policeman began.

Hannah knew he was taking in the state of the room. Her parents had done their best in the great clean-up but you wouldn't have to be Sherlock Holmes to work out what had gone on. The cops would guess they'd all been pissed, that memories would be hazy.

'Of course she's sure,' Dad snapped.

No, she wanted to scream, *no I'm not*. It was too difficult. She couldn't find the words. She didn't know where to start or even if she wanted to start at all. They wouldn't believe her. They'd wonder why it had taken her till Tuesday to report it and, if they did believe her, where would it lead? She couldn't bear people knowing about it and talking about it. What had she done? She should have kept quiet.

'Just tell us what happened, Hannah,' the police lady was saying. 'You don't have to take it any further and you don't need to press charges, not if you don't want to. Just tell us what happened.'

Hannah heard a sharp intake of breath from Dad. She sensed looks being exchanged.

'I'll make some tea,' Dad said, in the resigned tone of someone who'd been dismissed.

Hannah didn't dare look at him. She didn't want to see the anger, the hurt and confusion on his face all over again. As Dad got up, the police lady came over and took his seat next to Hannah on the settee.

'Maybe you could just tell me about the party,' she said. 'Your mum tells me it wasn't planned, that it was something your friends arranged.'

Hannah raised her head a little, looking at the cops properly for the first time. The policewoman looked older than Hannah had first thought. She was maybe in her late-thirties or early-forties. She was much older than the man anyway, who was sitting in the armchair, a notebook in his hand. The man with the boring name – PC Steven Smith, he'd said. He was youngish, maybe only mid- or late-twenties, and he looked familiar. She'd definitely seen him before. He had the kind of face you noticed. Good-looking in a slightly false, male-model sort of way, as if he should have been a TV cop, not a real one.

'Take your time,' the woman said.

She was in uniform too. Kate Campbell. Another PC, so they hadn't exactly sent their most senior cops round. This was probably all a boring routine to them; stupid drunken, drugged-up kids getting themselves into trouble.

'Tell me who arrived first,' PC Campbell said, smiling as she spoke, nodding encouragement. 'Just the party,' she added, 'you can stop at any time, all right?'

She smiled again as Hannah began to talk. Explaining how it started was easy enough. Going over what she'd already told her parents and, when the memories got hazy, when she started stumbling or faltering, the policewoman gently prompted, asking questions. But the story was bubbling out all confused and out of sequence. There were so many questions she couldn't answer. Details she honestly couldn't remember, like what she'd been drinking.

'We think her drink may have been spiked,' Mum said.

'No! I've told you. It was nothing like that. Jackie made it up!'

'How can you be sure?' Mum said.

'All right,' said the policewoman as Dad came back, handing out mugs of tea, 'let's just stick to what Hannah remembers, what she's sure about. So you think you may have blacked out, upstairs in your room?'

'Maybe not passed out exactly, maybe I just fell asleep.'

She hadn't told them about what she'd seen, about Shane and Eden. Why not? Why had she missed that bit out?

'And when you came down from your room, do you know what time it was?'

'No, not really, one o'clock, maybe later, I really don't know.'

It was already sounding all wrong, like she couldn't remember anything, be sure about anything. Why was she telling them all this anyway, what was the point? She wasn't going to go any further. She couldn't. It would just cause a whole load of hassle, for nothing.

'And the house was empty, you said – everyone had gone – yes?'

'Everyone except Zak,' Hannah said, glancing at Mum whose lips had tightened into a pale, thin line.

Dad moved from the position he'd taken up by the door. He crossed to Mum's chair, leaning against it, as if for support. His face was grey, completely grey. Hannah had never seen anyone look quite like that before. PC Smith glanced up from his notes and Hannah remembered where she'd seen him before. She'd been with Zak in his car once, when he'd been stopped for an allegedly 'routine check'.

Zak was always getting stopped. It was the sort of car the cops noticed, with its tinted windows, fancy lights, stupid exhaust and music constantly blaring out. The cop showed no sign of recognising her though. Why should he? He must stop dozens of lads with their girlfriends every week. Why should he remember her? He probably wouldn't even remember Zak.

'Go on,' said PC Campbell, 'what happened next?'

'Tell us, Hannah,' Mum urged, 'what happened with Zak?'

With every prompt Hannah could feel herself weakening, like she had no will of her own, no power to resist.

'He started on about the same old stuff, how much he loved me, how he didn't want us to split. I couldn't be bothered with it. I was too tired, I felt ill, all the mess, it was too much, I—'

'It's all right,' said the policewoman, 'you're doing really well.'

'I yelled at him to get out. Zak started yelling back, saying he was sick of me pissing him around, saying I didn't know what I wanted, calling me a—'

She stopped, not wanting to repeat the things he'd said.

'You know,' she continued, as the policewoman smiled at her again, 'calling me names and stuff because I wouldn't, because we hadn't ever – done it.'

'You mean you hadn't ever had sex with Zak?' PC Campbell said.

'Yes,' Hannah said, glancing at Dad. 'I mean no, we hadn't. We—'

She stopped. She wasn't going to go into details about what they'd done, how far they'd gone, how it wasn't enough for Zak. How he kept pressuring her.

'Anyway Zak completely lost it. He can be, you know, he can get really angry sometimes. He'd never got mad with me before though. I'd never seen him so ... I mean, I was scared, really scared. I thought he was going to hit me.'

She stopped as a slight movement over by the door caught her eye. She looked, blinked then looked again. He was standing there! Zak was standing there beyond the open doorway like her words had somehow conjured him up. She was going crazy, cracking up, hallucinating or something. He wasn't there, not really, he couldn't be. But the others saw him too.

'I wouldn't have done that,' he said. 'I'd never hit you. You know that. Why are you talking about this, what's going on?'

So he'd heard. How long had he been standing there? How had he got in? Dad must have left the door open. Zak was looking from Hannah to the police, to Dad then back again. Then, before Hannah could even think about answering, the room erupted in a blur of movement.

Dad lurched towards Zak. Zak stepped back and everyone except her stood up. The policeman pulled Dad out of the way then positioned himself between Zak and Dad. Hannah wanted to do something or say something but she couldn't. Everything was happening so quickly. Zak was looking around wildly as if he was about to run. The policeman was shouting, telling everyone to stay still and stay calm. He was looking at Zak as if he might have remembered him after all.

'What?' Zak snarled at Dad, who was still blocked by the cop. 'We had a row, that's all. I was out of order. But I wouldn't have hit her! I'd never hurt Hannah – no way!'

Dad launched himself forward again, pushing the cop out of the way.

'No!' Hannah shouted. 'Dad, stop, you've got it wrong. He didn't do anything.'

She wanted to get up, to stop him but her limbs felt heavy, frozen, paralysed almost. But it was OK. The policeman had regained his balance. He'd grabbed Dad, and the woman had somehow moved round next to Zak, her hand resting lightly on his arm.

'What?' said Zak again, shaking the cop's hand away. 'What's goin' on? If this is about the stuff I found.'

'It's not,' Hannah said. 'This isn't about you or the missing stuff. It's got nothing to do with you.'

They were all looking at her now. Her parents had got it wrong. Of course they had! She should have known what they'd think, what they must have thought from the start. She should have explained.

'What hasn't?' Zak said. 'Hannah?'

'It wasn't him,' Hannah yelled. 'Let him go, I don't want him here.'

'You're saying that he had nothing to do with—' Mum began.

'No! Get him out, get him out of here!'

The policewoman signalled to her colleague who let go of Dad and ushered Zak out. Hannah could hear raised voices from the direction of the kitchen near the back door.

'My colleague will just take a few details,' PC Campbell said, answering Hannah's unspoken question, 'in case we need to contact Zak later.'

'Later,' said Dad, pacing the room, 'you mean you're letting him go?'

'Unless Hannah tells us that he was involved in some way.'

'I already said, he didn't do anything!'

'Are you scared of him?' the policewoman asked, looking down at her.

'She's trying to protect him,' Mum said.

'No, I'm not! There's nothing to protect!'

Somewhere in the background, Zak was still shouting. Why didn't he just give PC Steven bloody Smith his name and address, answer any questions and get out?

'You're saying that Zak didn't do anything?' The policewoman said, sitting beside her, again. 'He didn't harm you in any way?'

'Of course he did!' said Mum. 'Tell her, Hannah. Tell her what you told us.'

The shouting had stopped. Hannah heard the back door slam then PC Smith came back, carrying Kyra's Nintendo, which he handed to Mum.

'Zak brought this,' the policeman said. 'He reckoned someone borrowed it.'

'Never mind that,' Dad said, 'where is he? You've let him go, haven't you?'

'For now,' Smith said. 'I took a short statement. He says he left shortly after Hannah woke up.'

'And you believed him?' said Dad. 'Look, if you're not going to do anything then I'll call someone who will.'

'It's true,' said Hannah. 'He left. He was yelling at me then he swings round and he starts thumping the wall really hard and his hand's bleeding and I'm screaming at him to stop and I'm really scared – but then he just stopped really suddenly, said he was sorry and walked out.'

'So what you told us,' said Mum, 'it wasn't true, nothing else happened?'

This was it. This was her chance to end it now.

'No,' she said, as calmly as she could, 'nothing happened. I made it up.'

'Why?' Mum whispered. 'Why would you say something like that?'

Attention-seeking, time-wasting, let them think what they liked. PC Smith sighed heavily, like he'd heard it all before. He started moving towards the door but the lady beside her didn't move at all.

'What did you mean, earlier,' the policewoman asked, 'when you said it wasn't him? Was there anyone else around?'

Hannah turned her head. Just let it drop, go away, why wouldn't they go away?

'What did you do when Zak left?' the policewoman went on. 'If anyone hurt you, Hannah, we need to know.'

No, they didn't. They didn't need to know anything else. She'd just have to handle it, get over it, deal with it herself, like she'd meant to do.

'Whatever happened, Hannah,' PC Campbell was saying, 'whoever it was, you need to tell us. We can help you.'

Why did she have to talk that way? Her words were quiet, coaxing, like she was some sort of hypnotist. Perhaps she'd been on a course or something; victim counselling! Maybe they hadn't just sent any old cops round. Maybe this one was trained to draw things out, make you say what you didn't really want to say.

'It's obvious what happened and who it was,' Mum said.

No, she couldn't let them believe that about Zak, but how could she tell them the truth?

'Just tell us, Hannah, in your own way,' PC

Campbell was saying, like it was some sort of religious chant.

The woman was good, far too good and, before Hannah really knew what she was doing, before she could work it all out, she was telling them everything, or almost everything.

10

The lights seemed to have stayed on red forever. Zak tapped the steering wheel waiting for them to change, wondering what was going on with Hannah and why the police wouldn't tell him anything. He didn't know the woman but he knew PC Smith and knew what a slimy bastard he was.

Smith hadn't been around the area long, only a year or so, if that, but he was the sort of cop Zak and everyone else noticed. He was always lurking in town picking on anyone wearing a hood or a baseball cap, like headwear was a crime. And when he wasn't hassling kids, he was stopping cars for no good reason that Zak could see.

'Oh, come on, change for Christ's sake,' Zak yelled at the red light.

The light ignored his instruction so Zak tilted his head against the headrest and drifted back to Hannah's. When he'd first seen the police car outside the house, he'd been sure it was about the damage and the missing stuff. He'd known it was crazy to go in. With *his* track record they were bound to jump to some wrong conclusion or other, but then when he'd pushed the door and it opened, it had just been too tempting.

Even so, he hadn't intended to hang around. Maybe just dump the Nintendo inside the door. He'd held that one item back, as an excuse to see Hannah, but he'd known it was a totally mad idea to start with and it got even madder with the cops snooping around.

Zak stopped tapping the steering wheel and nibbled one of the nails on his right hand that had been annoying him. He couldn't believe he'd been so stupid, that he hadn't just dumped the Nintendo and left. Instead, he'd hovered in the kitchen, then headed to the lounge to see if he could hear anything, get some idea what was kicking off or how much they knew. That's when he'd heard his name!

Behind him a horn beeped. The lights had finally changed. He pulled his nail away from his mouth, stuck his finger up and pulled off. He accelerated fast, leaving the car behind stuck and its driver cursing, as the lights changed again.

The cops, Zak reflected, had barely been interested in the Nintendo he'd left on the kitchen table and they hadn't asked about the TV. So, like Hannah had said, it wasn't about the missing stuff. Something else had happened. The way Hannah's dad had gone for him, like he wanted to kill him, wasn't because of a television or a games console.

The same thoughts kept playing over and over in Zak's mind, filling his head with a dark mist so he could barely concentrate on where he was driving. He needed to get home, take something to calm him down. He turned on his CD loud but it didn't help. Something had happened with Hannah, someone had hurt her. He lifted his hand from the wheel, wiped the sweat from his face and opened the window. The rain had finally stopped properly and the sun was blazing again, like the weather was as mixed-up as his head. He tried to remember exactly what he'd heard but it was all in fragments and he struggled to pick out whole sentences.

'Dad, stop, you've got it wrong. He didn't do anything.'

'You're saying, he had nothing to do with...'

Within minutes Zak wound up the window, feeling suddenly cold, very cold.

'We're following up an allegation.'

Once he'd remembered it, the word 'allegation' refused to go away. There'd been something in the way they'd said it. He searched around in his mind, in the mist, in the blackness, drawing out other bits of conversation. He pictured the looks on their faces, and the evidence was suddenly all pointing to one thing, one impossible thing.

He gripped the steering wheel tight, swung the car right round the mini-roundabout and put his foot down. He didn't know whether anyone had seen Hannah in the early hours of Sunday morning, after he'd left the party, but he knew someone who might. He turned left then left again and headed towards Lee Broadhurst's estate.

Now Zak's mind had settled on Lee, it was all starting to make more sense. He'd known there was something dodgy about Lee's story on Sunday night but he hadn't bothered too much then. By Monday he'd got all the stuff back and that was all that had mattered. He hadn't really cared who'd nicked it – until now.

'Shit, bollocks!' he yelled as a cyclist suddenly appeared in front of him.

He braked, slammed his horn and swore again as the cyclist wobbled off round the corner. He needed to stop thinking, to just concentrate on his driving but a question kept rolling round his mind... *What if they hadn't just nicked stuff, what if they'd done something else?*

He made a final left turn into Lee's estate. It wasn't far from Hannah's but it was like a different universe; a poorer, shabbier universe. He drove past a block of flats and a row of semi-boarded-up shops on Heron Road and turned sharp right into Raven Close with its tiny modern houses packed close together.

Every time Zak came here he was struck by how stupid all the street names were. Most of the people on this estate had never even seen a heron and Lee wouldn't recognise a raven if it perched on the end of his nose and started pecking his eyes out. He pulled up by number six, got out, strode towards the door and pressed the bell. It was nearly midday but Lee would probably still be in bed. His mum and grandparents would be on their market stall. Lee was supposed to help out but he never did. Lee didn't like work of any sort.

'Come on!' Zak said, pressing the bell for the second time.

He carried on pressing until the door opened.

'All right,' Lee said, still zipping up his jeans as he opened the door.

Zak pushed his way in, slamming Lee against the wall. There was no point wasting time. Lee was a bit younger than him and smaller so Zak knew he wouldn't have much trouble.

'So,' Zak said, 'tell me again. This guy that you don't really know brings you the stuff and tells you to look after it?'

'Yeah that's—'

'Bollocks, Lee!'

'Yer got it back, didn't you? Yer said that's all that mattered.'

'I've changed my mind.'

'He'll kill me if I say 'owt.'

'And yer think I won't?' said Zak, applying a bit more pressure to Lee's throat.

He didn't squeeze too hard. He never left any marks, not unless he had to. He waited a moment then eased off so Lee could talk.

'He made me get Granddad's van.'

'Who's he?'

Lee shook his head until Zak slammed it back against the wall. Zak could guess who Lee meant. He'd sort of known all along, but he waited to hear him say it. He needed to be sure.

'Jed!' Lee yelped. 'He said there was loads of stuff just waiting to be lifted. He said we could get in through the broken window but we didn't have to. The back door was unlocked, it was easy!'

'And what did you do to Hannah?'

'Nothin', we didn't even see Hannah, we didn't see no one!'

Lee groaned, doubling up as Zak kneed him in the groin. Zak could feel the mist in his head getting darker, heavier all the time. He didn't care any more if he left any marks, if he hurt Lee or not. He had to know and he had to find out soon – before he did something really crazy.

'The truth, Lee,' Zak said. 'I want the truth.'

It was sweltering when Zak got back in his car. He opened the windows and set off without really being sure where he was going although the car seemed to be heading roughly in the direction of Jed's hostel. He decided to go with his instincts, or the car's instincts, even though dealing with Jed would be tricky – on the grounds that Jed was a total psycho and not so easy to handle as Lee. Besides, Zak was pretty sure Lee would be calling Jed right now, warning him, making sure they were both going to tell the same story.

'Lying bastards the pair of them,' Zak muttered, but then again, Lee's story could be true.

'The house were dead quiet,' Lee had said, 'When me and Jed got back there.'

'What time was it?'

'I dunno, honest I don't,' Lee had squealed. 'Jed went back to the hostel after the party but they'd locked up, so he couldn't get in. He was pissed off, I reckon, so he came round here and starts going on about taking the van back to Hannah's.'

Zak tried to work out how long it would have taken for Jed to get to the hostel, go to Lee's, get the van and back to Hannah's but it was hard to say.

'Hannah weren't there when we turned up,' Lee had said. 'Not downstairs anyway, there was no one!'

They'd guessed she must have gone to bed but they hadn't looked, hadn't checked – they were just glad no one was around.

'We just grabbed stuff from rooms where the doors were open. You know, easy stuff – easy to move, easy to sell.'

'Yeah,' Zak had growled, 'I know.'

Zak turned left at another mini-roundabout. He wasn't far from the hostel now so he tried to think quickly, going over everything Lee had told him. They'd looked for money, of course, but Hannah's parents hadn't been stupid enough to leave any lying around. They might have taken more stuff, Lee had said.

'We were back downstairs and thinking about some of the big stuff like that massive TV in the lounge, but then we heard someone moving around upstairs.'

'Hannah?' Zak had asked.

'No,' Lee had said, in between rubbing his groin and whining about how much his head hurt. 'Why are you askin' anyway, what's going on?'

'You don't need to know, just answer.'

'It weren't Hannah!'

'You sure? You didn't see her, you didn't do nowt, cos if I find out you even bloody looked at her!'

Zak could feel his heart thumping faster, louder, just thinking of those two going anywhere near Hannah.

'I've told you,' Lee almost screamed, 'no! We knew it weren't Hannah cos we heard him cough.'

'Him? Who?'

'I dunno, do I? We didn't hang around to look. We got out of there quick.'

'You sure there was someone, you're not making this up?'

Lee had doubled over again at that point. Probably something to do with Zak's fist making contact with his gut but he'd eventually managed to splutter the next bit.

'We thought it was you! That's why we left. We knew you'd kill us if you came down and found us there.'

'Me, you frickin' moron, why would it be me?'

'Well, you know — you and Hannah.'

'Yeah, sure, Lee, me and Hannah, as if!'

But, Zak wondered as he drew up outside the hostel, if it wasn't him and if Lee was telling the truth, who the bloody hell was it? And what exactly had he done? One thing was for sure, he was going to find out, if not from Jed then from someone else. And when he did, the guy was seriously dead – if Hannah's dad didn't find the bastard first.

He took a deep breath as he opened the car door. Jed was the one he needed to talk to first and that definitely wasn't going to be easy.

11

Hannah shivered as she followed the policewoman and her parents along a corridor and into a room. She'd seen enough cop programmes to know that this was a 'soft' interview suite. It was the kind reserved for victims or witnesses who'd volunteered to 'help the police with their enquiries'. The cream-painted walls were light and cheery with a couple of pictures. They were both abstract, with multi-coloured geometric shapes that made her eyes go funny as soon as she looked at them. So she looked away and let her eyes settle on a vase of flowers on the low table.

It was all meant to feel safe and relaxing, but how could it be with a camera pointing from the corner and a voice recorder next to the bloody flowers? She hadn't wanted to come but they'd said she must.

'You need to make a formal statement,' PC Campbell had said.

But there was something else as well. Something they needed to do, something she definitely didn't want to think about. She didn't want to go through with this, but her mother was already steering her towards one of the beige two-seater sofas. Mum sat down next to her and tried to hold her hand but Hannah pulled it away.

Dad sat alone on a matching beige chair to the side of them, his hands clenched together resting on his knees, the knuckles white, flecked with red. The policewoman had settled on another small sofa directly opposite her. Hannah didn't know where PC Smith had gone but his place had been taken by a woman in plain clothes, a DC or a DS or something.

She'd introduced herself soon after they'd arrived at the station but Hannah hadn't remembered the rank, just the name – Robson. Her mind wouldn't focus on anything properly. It was all moving too fast. She'd said too much and now they wanted her to say it all again. Or at least PC Kate Campbell did – and Dad.

'Of course she wants to press charges,' Dad had said, back at the house. 'You heard what happened, you heard what she said!'

Mum had been wavering by then, slumped in an armchair shaking her head, unable to believe it or accept it. And if Mum barely believed her, who would? It would have been different if she'd said it was Zak. Mum would have believed that easily enough. She'd even asked, more than once.

'Are you sure?' she'd said. 'Are you sure it wasn't Zak?'

Like it was the sort of thing you could be mistaken about! Or did Mum really think she'd stitch someone else up just to protect Zak or because she was scared of him or something? Hannah was suddenly aware of eyes looking at her as though someone had been talking to her, asked her something. The plain-clothes woman, Robson, was looking towards the voice recorder as if Hannah was expected to speak.

'The party,' Robson prompted, 'tell us what happened. You'd been left on your own for the weekend, yes?'

'She's sixteen,' Mum murmured, 'we thought it would be all right. Oh God, we shouldn't have left her. We should never have left her.'

'It's all right,' the detective said, although her tone was giving off a different message, 'you weren't to know. Just let Hannah tell us what happened.'

This time Hannah's account came out more smoothly, as if she'd rehearsed it or was reading

123

from a script. That's the way it felt; like she was in a play, acting a part, as if it was all happening to someone else. She was aware she was talking quickly, wanting to get it over with, finished, but her voice sounded distant, detached and eventually it disappeared completely. She'd stopped talking, the script had run out and another voice was prompting.

'So how did you feel when Zak left?'

'I don't know. Upset, confused, a bit scared, I guess. He'd been so angry and I kept looking around at all the mess. I didn't know what to do, I felt ill. I didn't want to be on my own so I...'

'Yes?'

'I phoned him. I phoned Shane.'

She heard a sharp intake of breath from Mum who started to cry again, like she'd done back at the house the minute Hannah had mentioned Shane. This time, above the crying, Hannah heard Robson's voice. Why had she done it? Robson wanted to know, why had she phoned Shane, why not one of her other friends?

'It's all right,' PC Campbell said, in her oh-so-soft voice, when Hannah didn't answer. 'I know it's difficult but you're doing really well.'

'I just needed someone to talk to,' Hannah said, repeating what she'd told them back at the house.

She still hadn't mentioned seeing Shane and Eden together and it was too late to change her story now. Besides, it wasn't important, not really. She hadn't believed what Eden had said about Shane having second thoughts about Lucy. She hadn't got him round in the hope that they'd get back together. That wasn't what it was about. It wasn't!

'They'd always been good friends,' Mum confirmed, wiping her eyes with her hand, 'even before they started going out. We're quite friendly with Shane's parents. I mean he's...we've always thought...he's a nice lad.'

She looked at Hannah apologetically, guiltily almost, as she finished.

'But you're not with this Shane now; he's an ex-boyfriend?' Robson was saying, as if it was a genuine question, as if she didn't know.

Hannah nodded.

'Yes,' she said, as PC Campbell pointed towards the voice recorder. 'I was crying. I told him what had happened with Zak. He said he'd come straight round. He doesn't live far. That's one of the reasons I phoned him and not one of the others.'

She wasn't sure that was true. She hadn't really thought about calling anyone else. Shane was the one she'd wanted. But not in that way, not in the way he'd thought! Not then anyway, not when she was so upset, so confused.

'I just wanted to talk,' she said, 'I wanted to sort things out. But I couldn't, I was so tired. He helped me get upstairs and into bed. I was feeling dizzy – still drunk,' she admitted. 'He lay down next to me. It was OK. I didn't mind. I thought he was just helping me, looking after me. I trusted him.'

When had it changed? There'd been a kiss. She hadn't really remembered that before. So how had it started? Had Shane kissed her or – the memory pushed its way through the haze in her head.

'We kissed,' she said, leaving it unspecific, open. 'I was OK with that too, at first.'

That wasn't quite what she'd said earlier, at the house. Is that why she had to go through it all again? Were they trying to trick her or look for changes in her story? She knew how it sounded. It sounded like she'd encouraged him. Like she'd led him on – and it was true, in a way. It had felt OK, sort of natural, being together again but she hadn't intended to do anything. She hadn't!

'But then he started touching me,' she went on, 'and . . . I said, "No", I kept saying, "No" but he wasn't listening and I was tired and I tried to push him away but—'

It was happening again, like it had earlier, at the house. The words were seizing up in her throat, choking her. She was shaking and she couldn't stop the tears. Should she have tried harder, made him stop? Could she have done that? She could almost feel the physical weight of him now, lying on her, pushing into her, not listening, not caring.

'How could he do something like that to Hannah?' she heard her dad yell. 'He's supposed to be her friend! You heard her. She trusted him.'

Her mum's arm was round her shoulder. Her dad stood up. He started pacing the room, still shouting and Hannah was vaguely aware of some-one leaning forward, switching off the machine. It wasn't over though. When she stopped crying, if she stopped crying, they'd want to ask the same stupid questions they'd asked back at the house and probably more besides.

What exactly had she drunk? Were there any drugs involved? Had she ever had sex with Shane before? As if she could answer truthfully with her parents sitting there! What difference did it make anyway? None of it changed what he'd done. She could hear her dad who'd stopped shouting and was talking in whispers, now with the policewomen.

'So,' Dad was asking, 'what happens next?'

'It depends,' one of the women said. 'I'm afraid it can be quite difficult to prosecute in cases like this.'

'Like what?' Dad hissed. 'Are you saying Hannah's lying?'

'No, of course not, it's just that . . .'

Hannah barely needed to listen. She knew how hard it was to prove so-called date-rape and exactly how feeble it sounded. They'd already pointed out some of her mistakes. They'd done it gently, their voices dripping sympathy, but underneath she'd heard the doubt as they'd outlined what she'd done wrong. How she should have reported it straight-away, how she shouldn't have washed the clothes or the bedclothes. Not to mention the fact that she'd been drunk so her memory might be faulty.

'You mean you've made her go through all this for nothing,' said Dad. 'Is that what you're saying?'

'No, there might well be a case but first we need to get Shane's side of the story. We're going to send someone round there first thing tomorrow.'

'Tomorrow?' Dad said, 'why tomorrow? Why not now? And you think he's going to tell the truth do you?' Dad added, while Robson muttered something about workload and paperwork and priorities.

'Like I said, it can be difficult,' Robson was saying. 'If it comes down to his word against Hannah's.'

Would it come to that? She'd barely thought how Shane would feel when the cops turned up to see him, how he'd react, and what he'd say. 'Oh, God, I'm sorry.' That's what he'd said when he left. Sorry! Like sorry could change anything. She hadn't wanted to get him into trouble though, not really. She'd tried to bottle it up, push it away and pretend it didn't matter but she couldn't. And he shouldn't have done it, he should have stopped! He shouldn't have left her feeling used and dirty; a feeling that she couldn't wash away.

'Can I go now?' she asked. 'I want to go home.'

'Soon,' PC Campbell said. 'I promise. But we've arranged for you to have a medical examination, remember?'

The words were spoken quietly but they seemed to fill the room like they'd been blasted out on loud speakers. They'd warned her about this. They'd told her she'd have to see one of their doctors but she couldn't face it.

'No!' she heard herself crying.

PC Campbell leaned forwards, lightly touched her hand and stared at her in that intense way she had.

'You have to,' she said. 'Whatever else happens you need to see a doctor. We need to check that you're not pregnant, OK? And you need to be tested for any possible infection.'

The words were still quiet, spoken softly and calmly but they felt so cold, so blunt. Infection. Pregnancy. She hadn't thought of anything like that, she'd barely had time. Now at least one of them seemed terrifyingly possible.

'We can arrange for a counsellor too,' said Robson. 'I think we might be able to get someone today, after you've seen the doctor.'

'No,' Hannah said again, but she said it quieter this time, knowing it was all going to happen anyway.

She'd lost the will to fight. It was all out of her control.

12

Zak groaned as he eased himself down onto the settee. His dad put a tray on the table next to him.

'I told you, I don't want nothing,' Zak said, but changed his mind when he saw the two white tablets.

He swallowed the painkillers and took a sip of the coffee, the heat of the mug burning into his split lip. His dad picked up the small bowl of cold water and the piece of kitchen towel off the tray then handed them to him.

'Bathe it,' he said.

Dad wasn't talking about the lip. He was talking about the mess that used to be Zak's right eye. Zak sat forward a bit and groaned again as a sharp pain ripped across his chest as though one of his ribs had cracked, which it probably had.

'You need to see a doctor,' Dad said.

'No, I don't. I'll be fine.'

His dad sighed, as he often did around Zak.

They were both used to this ritual, though it usually happened on a Friday or Saturday night, not in the middle of a fairly sunny Tuesday afternoon.

'I don't suppose you're going to tell me what happened,' Dad said.

'I got in a fight.'

'I can see that! Was it at work?' Dad said.

'No, I'm on a day off.'

'But you said you were working at eleven.'

'I lied, all right?'

His dad didn't respond other than with another small sigh, which told Zak that Dad wasn't in a confrontational mood. Unlike Jed, who'd gone completely ballistic, totally schizoid, even for him. He'd kicked off before Zak had even mentioned Hannah! Jed, it seemed, had found out that Zak had nicked the stuff back and he wasn't happy about it. Zak dabbed the cold water on his eye.

'It's not too bad,' Zak said, as he blinked the water away. 'I can still see.'

'So who was it this time?'

'Just Jed,' Zak said, deciding there was no point lying.

'I don't know why you hang around with him,' Dad said. 'I mean it's not the first time you've been in a fight with him, is it?'

'It's what Jed does,' Zak said, 'fists first, questions later. It's usually OK but he completely lost it today. It took half a dozen of the hostel guys to drag him away.'

Zak laughed at the memory of Jed swearing and kicking out at the care workers, but the laugh hurt his mouth and sent another sharp pain shooting across his chest. His dad looked on, frowning, as the laugh mutated into a groan.

'Did they call the police?'

'No way! They won't do nothing about it, they never do. Well, they might fill in a couple of incident forms and make Jed go to counselling again or something but they won't call the cops. Too many fights, too much trouble and the hostel gets shut down so they only call the cops if there's knives or stuff.'

'Knives!' Dad said.

'Yeah, don't panic. I don't carry and neither does Jed, thank God, but some of 'em do.'

Dad shook his head as if he didn't really want to know what went on in Zak's world.

'You feeling any better?' he eventually asked.

'Yeah, I'm good.'

'I'll go and finish the lawn then,' Dad said. 'I don't suppose you want to come and sit outside?'

133

'No, I'm gonna try and get some sleep.'

'Well, I'm outside if you need me,' Dad said, his voice tired, resigned.

Zak watched him shuffle out. He couldn't help noticing how old Dad looked these days. He wasn't even fifty yet but his hair, or what little he had left, was already going grey and there were deep wrinkles round his eyes and mouth.

'Yeah I know,' he said, looking at all the pictures of Mum that his dad insisted on keeping shrine-like around the house, 'I don't help.'

Zak had lost count of the number of fights he'd been in, times the cops had been round and all the rows he'd had with Dad. But, on the other hand, he'd never actually been charged with anything, he'd never been in prison. He worked, he'd always had a job since he left school and he always turned up on time no matter what he'd been doing the night before. He knew he'd go in tomorrow even though his ribs would still be sore and his eye a mess. He wasn't lazy like Lee or a total waster like Jed.

'I'm not that bad!' he told the pictures.

Zak put his legs up on the settee and closed his eyes so he wasn't tempted to look at the photos, wasn't tempted to talk to them again! He shuffled, trying to get comfortable, trying not to think too much. He could be better, he knew that. He'd been sort of getting there when he'd been with Hannah, he was sure. The thought of Hannah made him open his eyes and sit up. He needed to find out what was happening with her but he didn't know how. He got his phone out, found Clare's number, stared at it for a while but didn't call it because his eyes were already starting to close.

'You should talk to your dad, you know, Zak.'

'Uh, what?' he said, opening his eyes, looking round then down at his phone.

It was his mum's voice he'd heard. Or thought he'd heard. Only he couldn't have. He must have been dreaming. He looked at the photos, which all seemed to be looking back at him but none of them were talking. He massaged the top of his cheekbone, underneath his sore eye, which had gone all cloudy. He blinked, trying to get the vision back.

'Just offer to help him in the garden, spend a bit of time with him, talk to him,' he heard the voice say.

Zak leaped up, staring round, and yelped as a pain tore across his ribs. His vision was back clear enough but what the hell was going on with his ears? He rubbed the side of his head, wondering if he had concussion and whether Jed had hit him harder than he'd thought. He walked over to the far wall, leaned forwards and peered into the mirror. His eye wasn't too bad, really. A bit blood-shot and bruised underneath but it would be fine in a day or two. He'd seen worse, but what about the damage you couldn't see? The kind of damage that made you hear voices.

Drugs could do that to you too but Zak didn't want to think about that. He didn't want to sleep either. Not now, not in this room. He shuddered and rubbed the top of his arms. Imaginary or not, maybe the voice was right. Maybe he should get out, do something to take his mind off stuff.

The pain tugged at his chest as he straightened up away from the mirror. He wasn't exactly in any state to push a lawn mower around but he could do some of the lighter stuff. 'Yeah, all right,' he told the photos, 'I'm going.'

Dad had just emptied the lawn-mower tray and was tipping the grass onto the compost heap. The lawn looked neat, for once, but there weren't many flowers left in the borders now. Dad looked up and smiled as Zak approached.

'Are you OK?'

'Yeah, just hallucinating, hearing voices, that sort of stuff,' Zak mumbled.

'Sorry, what?'

'I said I'm not too bad, need any help?'

'Well, I was thinking of sanding down that bench and repainting it. Not that anyone sits out here very much but...'

'Yeah, we can do that.'

Offering to help was easy enough and sanding the bench didn't pull on Zak's ribs too much, but the conversation wasn't exactly going well. His dad was doing his best, talking about cars, which was about the only interest they had in common these days, but that's as far as it went. Zak found it impossible to talk about personal stuff and he couldn't really talk to Dad about the one thing he wanted to talk about – Hannah.

Dad had never met Hannah. He didn't even know Zak had been going out with her because Zak had never told him. So when they'd finished with cars they worked in silence until Zak's phone blared out. He stopped what he was doing and answered it.

'Yeah, all right,' he snarled. 'I suppose so. I'll be there in twenty minutes. Yeah, fine, I told you, I'll do it.'

'Who was it?' Dad asked.

'The boss. Two people have phoned in sick. He

wants me to cover till ten o'clock. It's true,' he added as he saw his dad's look of disbelief. 'He always phones me when he's bloody stuck, which is nearly every day cos he's opening virtually twenty-four/seven over summer.'

'You're in no state to go to work.'

Zak knew his dad was right. He knew he ought to go to the doctors or A&E or something, check out the voices.

'I'll be fine. I need the money and with any luck I'll get part of tomorrow off instead. We'll finish the bench then, OK? And I'll come back tonight after work.'

He headed inside but even when he came back out in his work clothes, the questioning look was still there. His dad didn't believe he was going to work. He never believed anything these days. Zak couldn't really blame him but occasionally, just occasionally, like now, he happened to be telling the truth.

13

Shane squeezed a big dollop of gel onto his hand and rubbed it in his hair. He peered into the bathroom mirror, pulling strands of hair into little spikes at the front. Great, just the way Lucy liked it.

'Oh, bugger,' he said as he heard the doorbell.

She was here already! He glanced at his watch then shoved his hands under the tap to get the gel off, as the doorbell carried on ringing.

'All right,' he muttered, 'I'm coming.'

He checked his watch again. Lucy was well early. Desperate to see him, obviously! He'd sort of known she couldn't stay mad at him for long. He smiled at his reflection as he grabbed a towel and dried his hands. He was just about to dart out when he realised the bell had stopped ringing.

Good, Mum had answered it. That gave him time to do his teeth so Lucy wouldn't start going on about his stinky breath again. No point giving her stuff to moan about. Finally, after about a million phone calls and texts, she'd stopped going on about the party! He picked up his toothbrush then put it down again. Nah, it was too much trouble. Instead he took a swig of mouthwash, swirled it round and spat it out.

All this fuss for a Wednesday-morning shopping trip! He was only going cos Lucy kept pestering him. 'Aw, go on, Shane. I hate shopping on my own.' If she'd only known what he'd had to go through with Dad!

'If you worked for someone else you wouldn't be able to snake off for the day,' Dad had moaned last night when Shane mentioned it. 'You need to start taking your commitments seriously, Shane!'

'My commitments, what's it got to do with me? It's you who's taken on all the extra work.'

'To pay for your skiing trip, Shane, remember? So the least you can do is help!'

Shane bared his teeth as he did a final check in the mirror. It was all right for Lucy. She didn't have to work at all cos she got loads of money off her dad. 'Guilt money' Lucy called it but it didn't stop her taking it and dragging Shane round the shops with her. Oh, well, he'd talked Dad round in the end, so now he had a whole morning of lurking outside changing rooms to look forward to. How good was that?

'Shane,' his mum shouted, 'are you still up there?'

Daft question, she knew exactly where he was so he didn't bother answering. He just picked up his jacket from the bathroom floor, put it on and headed off. Halfway down the stairs he realised it wasn't Lucy at the bottom at all. It was two cops standing with Mum in the hallway. Images of falling ladders flashed through his mind. Dad had gone out at about seven to make up for not having a helper. Maybe he'd been half-asleep. Maybe he hadn't even got to work. Maybe he'd crashed the van. Oh God!

'Is it Dad?' Shane said as he stumbled down the last few stairs. 'Has something happened to Dad, has he had an accident?'

'No,' Mum said, looking from him to the two cops, 'there's nothing wrong with your dad. They want to talk to you.'

'Me?'

His stomach instantly started churning, like he was on some theme-park ride. But it was crazy. He hadn't done anything wrong. He wasn't in any bother. There was nothing to be scared of.

'Shane, what's going on?' Mum asked.

'I don't know – nothing! I haven't done nothing!'

'Shane's never been in any trouble,' Mum murmured.

'Can we go through here,' the older of the two cops said, pointing to the open lounge door.

'Er, yes, of course,' Mum said.

'Why?' Shane asked. 'What's going on, what's this about? I don't remember robbing any banks recently.'

He smiled as he said it but the cops didn't smile back. The younger one was frowning slightly. The older one showed no expression at all. He had one of those battered, lived-in sort of faces, with a funny-shaped nose that looked as if it had been broken a few times. He was big too, like he was an ex-heavyweight boxer or something.

'Just come through and sit down please,' Boxer Man said.

He led the way into the lounge while the younger one held back until Shane and Mum got inside, as if he was barring their escape route. Mum sat on the chair at the computer, where she'd been working earlier, and swung it round to face the middle of the room. Shane didn't feel like sitting but Boxer Man kept staring at him so he perched on the arm of a chair.

'I'm Sergeant Woodhead,' Boxer Man said, as soon as Shane sat down, 'and this is PC Smith.'

'Steven Smith,' the younger one said, as if he was setting himself up to be 'good cop' against Boxer Man's 'bad cop', just like on TV. 'We just need to ask you a few questions, all right?'

Well, no, it wasn't all right, but as Woodhead asked his first question, Shane slid from the arm and settled into the chair. Hannah's party, was that all they wanted to talk about? By the looks they'd been giving him, he'd expected to be accused of global terrorism at the very least. But, no, they wanted to know if he'd been to a party.

'Yeah, I was there,' he said, 'but only for an hour or so.'

'That's right,' his mum said, 'we were still awake when Shane came back so it can't have been much later than eleven.'

'And what did you do when you came home?' Sergeant Woodhead asked.

'I went to bed,' said Shane.

'So you didn't go out again?'

'Er, no,' said Shane, 'why? I mean I know there was some trouble and some stuff got nicked but—'

'You didn't tell me anything was stolen,' Mum said, looking at him as if he was supposed to tell her every detail of his life. 'You just said there'd been a bit of bother. I mean I would have phoned Hannah's parents if I'd known.'

'Yeah, exactly,' Shane muttered.

His parents didn't see Hannah's parents much since the split but they still talked. 'Well, we don't want things to get awkward, do we?'

'It was more than a bit of bother,' Sergeant Woodhead said, glaring at Shane. 'The house was completely wrecked but this isn't about that – or the stolen goods. They've got most of them back.' He paused. 'This is about an allegation of a serious sexual assault.'

'What?' said Mum. 'I mean, who? What's it got to do with Shane?'

Shane sat forward on his chair, as the sergeant answered Mum's first two questions.

'Bloody hell!' Shane said. 'No way! Hannah! You saying someone raped Hannah? No, no way, that's not right. It can't be.'

'Oh my God,' his mum said. 'I don't believe it.'

'And you're sure you didn't go out again after you got home, Shane?' said the sergeant.

'No, of course he didn't!' said Mum, while Shane was still trying to take in what he'd heard.

They were wrong. They had to be wrong.

'Hannah says he did. She says he went back there after the party, in the early hours of Sunday morning.'

'That's rubbish,' said Mum, 'why would she say that?'

Shane looked at his mother then at the cops. *Oh shit, there was no point denying it. Not now, not if Hannah had already told them. He should never have lied in the first place. It was stupid. He should have told them the truth. He had nothing to hide – not really.*

'It's true,' Shane said. 'She phoned me. She was upset. The house was wrecked, like you said. She'd had a massive row with a guy called Zak, she was upset,' he said again, 'she didn't know what to do and she asked me to go round.'

'In the middle of the night,' Mum said, 'and you went, without even telling us!'

'You were asleep by then and I had to go, she was completely like hysterical! She was on her own. She sounded pretty drunk, sort of desperate. I was worried about her. I felt sorry for her. I couldn't just ignore her,' he said, rattling out the reasons that had all seemed so obvious at the time.

'So what happened when you went round?' Woodhead asked.

Oh, bollocks, what a mess! He didn't know what to say. He didn't know how much Hannah had told them or even why she'd told them at all.

'I tried to calm her down,' he said, 'I told you! She was in a complete state. But she didn't say nothing about no one doin' anything like that to her, I swear. She just said her and Zak had a row!'

The cops were both staring at him, wanting more. What was he supposed to say?

'And then what happened?' Woodhead asked.

'I helped her get upstairs, into bed.'

'Then?'

The truth, just tell them the bloody truth! But he couldn't, he wouldn't, not if he didn't have to. It was all too crazy, too messy.

'I waited till she fell asleep then I came home.'

'That's all?'

'Yeah, I mean . . .'

He paused as a memory came back to him. Something he hadn't thought was important at the time but maybe it was. Maybe it was the clue they needed.

'I thought I heard someone,' he said. 'Before I left I went to the loo and while I was in there I thought I heard something, someone downstairs. But when I got down there, there was no one, nothing. So I thought I must have imagined it. But I looked around anyway. I checked. I even locked the back door before I left out the front.'

The two cops were looking at each other, frowning as he spoke.

'Oh God,' he said, as his stomach started turning over again, 'are you saying someone was in the house? I left someone there with Hannah and they . . .'

'No,' said Sergeant Woodhead, staring at him, 'that's not what we're saying and that's not what Hannah's saying either. She didn't mention anyone else,' he continued, his voice getting quieter. 'She alleges that you were the one who assaulted her.'

'Me!' Shane yelled, jumping up, as his mother shrieked and also got up sending the computer chair spinning round and round. 'No way, that's crazy, you've got it wrong!'

'That's ridiculous,' his mother said. 'How could Hannah say that, how could anyone even think that Shane would—?'

She grabbed hold of the chair, steadied it and sat down again, taking deep breaths.

'I think we need to continue this down at the station,' Woodhead said.

No, no way, this was just bloody mental.

'You're arresting him?' Mum said, snatching up her phone. 'I'm phoning his father. We need a solicitor. This is outrageous. Shane wouldn't do something like that, not to Hannah, not to anyone!'

'Shane's not under arrest,' Woodhead said, 'but we would like him to make a formal statement and you can, of course, phone your husband and a solicitor.'

Shane stood rigid, holding onto the back of the chair while his mum phoned Dad. He could hear Dad shouting as Mum tried to explain.

'I'm sure it's all a mistake,' she said, 'just phone the solicitor and meet us at the station. We'll get it cleared up, it's all a mistake.'

It was more than a mistake it was a total nightmare. It wasn't happening, it wasn't possible. Somehow, some way, someone had got it well wrong. The cops had stood up by the time Mum had finished her call and were waiting while she shoved stuff in her handbag; phone, keys, tissues and a pen.

OK, he could explain it, he realised. There was still time. They didn't have to go to the station. He could clear this up now. He could do what he should have done all along – tell the full story, tell the truth.

'Look,' he said, 'I don't know what's gone on or what Hannah's said but you've got it mixed up. We had sex, right, but I didn't assault her, no way. Ask her! Ask Hannah properly, she'll tell you.'

'Shane!' Mum screeched, gripping her handbag to her chest like it was some sort of comfort blanket. 'You don't mean that?'

'I'm sorry,' said Shane, looking from his mum to the cops, 'it shouldn't have happened but it did. She was really coming onto me, saying how she still loved me. We'd both been drinking. You know what it's like! It just happened but she wanted to, I swear I didn't—'

'Don't,' said his mother, starting to cry. 'Don't say anything else.'

'I'm telling the truth!' he said, as the cops started to herd them out. 'I mean she even sent me a text on Sunday afternoon. Hannah sent *me* a text, sayin' we needed to talk or something. I deleted it in case Lucy saw it but you can check, can't you? I mean, why would Hannah do that? Why would she text me if she thought I'd assaulted her? It's Wednesday now for Christ's sake! Did it take her four bloody days to decide?'

'Shane!' his mother warned.

'Well, it's obvious what happened,' Shane went

on, ignoring his mother's warning. 'She woke up, sobered up, decided she'd made a mistake and tried to blame it all on me. She might have said it to stop her parents goin' on about the house! That could be it, couldn't it? Attention seeking and stuff?'

Nobody answered him. Nobody seemed to be listening. The younger cop opened the front door. Shane followed him out towards the police car, outside the gate, because he didn't know what else to do. This was completely crazy. He glanced round to see if Mum was following and noticed old Mrs Yates next door peering out of her window.

Over the road Mr Singh was doing something with his roses. Tina two doors along was playing ball with her three kids. Mrs Lucas was coming down the road towards them with her stupid snappy Jack Russell, tugging on its lead. All living their lives like this was an ordinary day!

Well, not that ordinary. They'd found something to liven things up cos they were all staring as he walked towards the cop car. Even the bloody dog seemed to be staring. Then, just as Shane was about to get into the car, he heard someone call his name. He looked towards the other end of the street. Lucy was hurrying towards them. Oh God, he'd forgotten all about Lucy and the bloody shopping!

'Shane,' she said again as she drew close, 'what's going on? Are you OK?'

'It's nothing,' he said, trying to force the words out. 'It's nothing. I'll be back soon. I'll phone you.'

'But what's happening – has there been an accident or what?'

'No, I've told you, it's nothing.'

'But—'

'Just leave it,' he snapped as he got into the car, 'and keep your mouth shut – don't tell no one about this. I'll explain when I get back.'

14

Hannah closed her eyes, aware that Mum was still in the room, and focussed on making her breathing heavy, regular, feigning sleep. Eventually she heard Mum go out and quietly close the door. Everything was done quietly now, everyone spoke softly, like lowering the volume of her life was supposed to help.

The doctor had spoken quietly too, yesterday afternoon, but it didn't make it any better. It didn't disguise what she'd had to do. They hadn't forced her but she'd agreed in the end. She'd known she had to. Suddenly retching, Hannah turned over and leaned towards the bowl that Mum had left at the side of her bed, but nothing came out apart from dribbles of pale bile. There was nothing in her stomach, nothing left to throw up.

She turned again and lay on her front, pressing her face into the pillow, trying to blot out images of the doctor and the clinical coldness of the examination room. The doctor had been nice. Everyone had been so bloody nice but it didn't help. It didn't stop her feeling dirty, degraded. They'd wanted her to see a counsellor too but she hadn't been able to face it.

Her parents had taken the rest of the week off work. God knows what reason they'd given but she doubted they'd told the truth. *'Sorry I won't be in this week – my daughter's been raped.'* Like you could just come out and say something like that!

Somehow life would have to go on. She'd have to eat, drink, talk to people but how could she do that? That's what the counsellor could help with, PC Campbell had said. Well not unless she was a bloody magician she couldn't.

Hannah heard her bedroom door click open. She kept her head buried in the pillow.

'Hannah?'

Easing herself onto her side, Hannah opened her eyes and looked up. Kyra was standing by the bed, her arms rigid like she was standing to attention. Her hair was tied up in two ridiculous bunches, sticking out from either side of her head like huge floppy rabbit ears. She was wearing blue denim shorts and a white T-shirt with pink glittery butterflies on the front, sparkling with tiny sequins that made Hannah blink.

'Mum said not to disturb you.'

'So why did you?'

'I just wanted to see how you are,' she said, staring.

Her bottom lip started to tremble slightly as she spoke.

'OK, so you've seen, now bugger off. It's not a spectator sport.'

'I've been worried about you,' Kyra said.

'Yeah, well, that's really helpful, Kyra,' Hannah snapped. 'That's made me feel a whole lot better.'

'Can I get you anything?'

Hannah's head was throbbing. She desperately needed a couple of paracetamol but she wasn't going to ask Kyra.

'No.'

'Hannah,' Kyra said again.

Kyra moved closer to the bed, bending down, her arms outstretched like she was going to hug her. Before she knew what she was doing Hannah sat up, her arm lashing out, smacking into Kyra's almost-flat chest. Kyra yelped, stumbled backwards, regained her balance then ran from the room, crying.

Hannah flopped down. Why had she done that? It wasn't Kyra's fault. Kyra was only trying to help. There'd been a time when they got on well; for most of their lives, in fact. It had only really changed in the past couple of years when everything Kyra did, every word out of her mouth, seemed to irritate her. She should at least have let Kyra get the bloody tablets. Now she'd have to call Mum or get up and get them her herself. There'd be some in Mum's bathroom cabinet. That would be easiest.

Getting out of bed, her body felt heavy. Her head was even heavier and she was exhausted by the time she'd got to the bedroom door, which Kyra had left open. There was no sign of her sister. Oh well, at least Kyra hadn't gone whining to their parents. Their bedroom door was open and Hannah could see Mum and Dad were in there, talking. They were also blocking the route to their bathroom. She didn't want them fussing, questioning, so best to get the tablets from the kitchen drawer instead. There were at least three boxes in there. An image flashed into her head of her picking up all the boxes, taking them to her room, opening them and swallowing the tablets one by one.

As she stood there, trying to drive away the thoughts, she realised her parents weren't talking, they were arguing. She hadn't noticed at first because they weren't shouting. Their voices weren't even particularly loud but the tone was sharp, bitter.

'Look, I don't need this right now,' Dad said. 'What's the point of blaming each other? We need to think about Hannah, how we can help her, what we're going to do.'

'But we shouldn't have left her,' Mum was saying, as she'd said a dozen times before. 'Why didn't you stand up to her, why didn't you insist she went to Mother's? She listens to you!'

'No,' Dad said, 'she doesn't. She stopped listening a long time ago.'

No, that wasn't true! How could they say that? She'd listened to all their bloody rules, their warnings. She'd tried to do what they said. It wasn't her fault. The party wasn't her fault – none of it was.

'We're her parents, for God's sake,' Mum said, 'we should have made her listen.'

'Maybe we should,' said Dad, 'but this isn't helping! There was no way, no way on earth she was ever going to go to her gran's with Kyra. You know what she's like. She's stubborn, Hannah's always been stubborn. You can't make her do anything she doesn't want to do.'

'Well her so-called bloody friends did and *he* did, didn't he?'

Hannah moved away quicker than she wanted to move, quicker than she was really able to move. She just didn't want to hear her parents arguing any more, she couldn't bear to hear them talking about *it,* about what had happened. All she wanted was to get downstairs, get the tablets and get back to her room before they heard her moving around.

She approached the stairs and barely knew she'd put her foot forward before she realised there was nothing solid underneath. Her arms flailed as she tried to grab the rail but it was too late. She was falling.

15

As soon as Dad stopped the van, Shane clambered out of the back and hurried towards the house. He kept his head down, not looking to see if any of the neighbours were out spying – watching, wondering why the police had taken him away or why they'd let him go again. His parents were almost as quick. Mum, with her keys already out, was opening the door. All of them bolting inside, like criminals, like they had something to hide.

Well, they didn't. He hadn't been charged with anything, not yet anyway. And they couldn't! It was all a pack of total bloody lies! His parents didn't look so sure. Mum was white, totally white. Her eyes were hidden behind sunglasses cos one of her migraines had kicked off. It had got so bad in the police station that she'd had to go out. So she'd missed most of the crap him and Dad had had to listen to.

Mum dropped her keys on the table in the hall and leaned on the banister. She'd taken a couple of her special pills but they didn't seem to have helped.

'I'm sorry,' she said to Dad, 'I feel sick. I'm going to have to lie down.'

'It's all right,' Dad said, squeezing her arm. 'I'll bring you a drink.'

Shane went into the lounge and collapsed on the settee. He buried his head in the cushions, glad of some time to be on his own. It wouldn't last long though. Dad would be back soon and, somehow, he had to fend Lucy off.

She'd sent at least a dozen texts while he'd been with the cops. They'd all been sitting there waiting for him when he turned his phone back on. More had popped up as he looked so he'd switched it off again. He couldn't ignore her for ever though. He'd have to see her. Try to explain – only it wasn't that easy, as he'd found out with the police.

He sat up and threw the cushion onto the floor. *What was their problem? It was simple enough for God's sake! Hannah was lying.* He didn't know why, but when he'd tried to tell the cops they'd just twisted everything. They'd asked whether he was sure Hannah had consented, like he didn't know the bloody difference. Then raised their eyebrows when he said he was totally one hundred per cent sure!

They wanted him to remember every word he'd said, every move he'd made on Saturday night but he couldn't. You didn't remember every detail of your life like that. You never expected it to be tested. They'd even asked him *why* Hannah had agreed, like he was supposed to be telepathic or something.

'I dunno, do I? She was drunk.'

'So you took advantage of someone who was drunk?'

'She wasn't *that* drunk, not by then. She knew what she was doing. I didn't rape her, no way! And I've told you, I didn't start anything, *she* did! She kept going on about how much she missed me and stuff. Maybe she thought we were going to get back together.'

'So you let her believe you were still interested?' they'd asked as he struggled to remember, tried to explain exactly what had gone on.

'No, I never said that! I'd sort of kept away from her at the party. But Hannah seemed to think there might be a chance cos Eden had been telling her a whole load of rubbish earlier.'

'Eden?' PC Smith had said, frowning at him.

'This is another friend, someone who was at the party?'

'She's not a friend, she's a total bitch.'

'Shane!' Dad had yelped. 'This won't help.'

'Well she is! The stupid cow dropped me right in it.'

'Meaning?' someone had asked.

He'd known he was in a hole but he hadn't been able to see a way out so he'd told the truth, like you were supposed to do. He told them all about Eden. Who she was, how long he'd known her, how she'd never taken much notice of him before. He told them about Eden getting everyone round to Hannah's then getting bored, coming onto him even though she supposedly had a bloke and, finally, how Hannah had caught them together.

'Hannah didn't mention that,' one of the cops had said.

'Well it happened! It's true! Ask her, ask Eden!'

'Oh, we will,' Smith had said.

'Then Eden must have tried to wriggle out of it by telling Hannah we'd gone up there for a cosy little chat about her and me. That's what Hannah told me anyway. I mean, I don't know what Eden was up to in the first place. She's a total slag. It's all like a bloody game to her.'

Oh God, it had been so embarrassing sitting there with the cops, his dad and the solicitor all looking at him as if he was a cross between Casanova and Jack the Ripper. Like it was his fault girls came onto him! They'd thought he'd screwed Eden too and he'd ended up explaining that it hadn't gone that far and exactly what they'd done.

He took his phone out and switched it on. Then he rolled over on the sofa, curled up and groaned. It all sounded so sleazy when you had to spell it out. He hadn't even known what words to use, whether he was supposed to be technical, clinical or describe it as if he was talking to his mates. And all the time, they'd been staring at him, judging him.

The younger cop was the worst. He'd dropped all pretence of 'good cop' and kept glaring, scowling, frowning, like he wasn't human, like he'd never heard of people making out before. He was good-looking in a boring, clean-cut-copper sort of way so he must have had girlfriends or boyfriends or something. He must know what went on!

Shane uncurled, got up and started pacing the room. The cops had delved into everything, like how long he'd been going out with Hannah before they split and whether they'd been sleeping together.

'It's none of your business!'

But it seemed it was, so he'd told them the truth and known by their expressions that Hannah had told them something different; like she was some virgin-innocent probably. They'd gone on to ask why they'd split and how Hannah had reacted to him getting together with her best friend. The cops had looked at each other when he'd said it had been 'tricky' and that Hannah had pestered him for ages until she'd taken up with Zak.

He flopped onto the settee again and pulled a cushion over his face. OK, so it hadn't exactly made him sound like a saint – dumping Hannah not long before her GCSEs, going with three different girls, to some degree or other, within a couple of days of that bloody party – but none of that made him a rapist! Hannah was lying, end of story. Or at least it should have been but the cops weren't gonna drop it. They'd said he had to go back, when they'd had a chance to speak to Hannah again. He pulled the cushion from his face and held it to his chest as Dad came in.

'I've made you some tea,' Dad said, putting a mug on the table next to the sofa.

Great! Like a mug of tea was going to solve his problems. His phone bleeped again. It had been bleeping from the minute he'd switched it back on.

He abandoned his cushion completely, throwing it onto the floor, switched the phone off again and dumped it on the table next to the mug.

'Your mum's been sick,' Dad said, 'she's gone to bed.'

That happened with Mum's migraines. She didn't get them often but when she did they were bad and could knock her out for a day or more. They weren't just headaches; it was the whole flashing lights, throwing-up thing.

'I'm sorry,' Shane said, although he wasn't sure which part of this whole bloody mess he was apologising for. 'You believe me, don't you? Hannah's stitching me up. I didn't rape her, I'm not like that. I wouldn't do anything like that.'

'I know,' his dad said, shaking his head. 'It's proving it that's the problem.'

'It can't be that difficult,' Shane said. 'Her story doesn't make sense. She's lied about loads of things. It's obvious! I don't know why she's doing this,' he added. 'I mean I know why she might be mad at me. I know why she'd be upset – but this!'

He'd known Hannah for ever! They'd gone out together for over a year. He couldn't believe she'd just lie like this.

'Maybe she thinks she's telling the truth,' Dad said.

Shane was about to yell, to tell him not to be so bloody stupid but he didn't cos he realised Dad might just be right. Maybe Hannah was so screwed up with exams, that crazy party, Zak and everything else, she'd got totally confused, had a breakdown or something. Maybe all the stress had made her totally flip out. Could she have taken something that made her hallucinate, get her memories all mixed up? It wasn't like Hannah to do heavy drugs but who knew what might have gone on? Jackie had been putting it round that someone had been spiking drinks, so what if she was right? Could Hannah have taken stuff and not known?

'I need to see Hannah,' he said. 'I need to talk to her, make her tell them the truth, make her see what she's doing.'

'God no,' Dad said. 'That's the last thing you should do. If you so much as think about seeing Hannah, they'll do you for harassment or something. Promise me you won't go anywhere or do anything without telling me first.'

'I won't. I'm not completely stupid. I just thought—'

They both looked towards the house phone as it rang. Dad picked it up.

'Oh, Lucy,' he said, looking towards Shane, who shook his head. 'No, he's asleep at the moment. I'll get him to call you when he wakes up. No, it's nothing, honestly, nothing to worry about.'

Right answer for Lucy but totally, totally wrong. If Hannah didn't change her story there was everything to worry about.

16

Hannah stood up and limped a few paces from the sofa to the armchair, just to see if she could, then sat down again.

'I really think I ought to call the doctor,' Mum said.

'No, I'm fine.'

She wasn't fine. Her back was aching, her wrist felt sore and her right knee had begun to swell. But nothing was broken and she didn't want to see another doctor, not now, not ever.

'You gave us such a fright when we heard you scream,' Mum said.

'I'm sorry.'

'No, don't be silly,' Mum said, kneeling beside her, 'that's not what I meant.'

'I don't know what happened,' Hannah said. 'I just missed the stair. I wasn't concentrating.'

She'd said all that a dozen times already, in the

hour or so since her parents had picked her up from the bottom of the stairs. She'd have to stop repeating it or Mum would think she'd got concussion or something. But she needed to make sure Mum knew she hadn't done it deliberately. That she hadn't hurled herself downstairs in some pathetic attempt to end it all. OK, so she'd thought about taking tablets, too many tablets, sure, but in that moment, as she fell, she'd known she didn't want to die. She was going to get through this; somehow she was.

Her mum just kneeled there, shaking her head slightly, as though she couldn't believe any of this was happening, as though she couldn't understand how it could keep getting worse and worse. Dad appeared in the doorway.

'I've phoned that counsellor,' he said, 'and cancelled the appointment. I'm not sure she quite believed the reason. She offered to come round here but I said no. I guessed you wouldn't want to...'

His voice trailed.

'Thanks,' Hannah said.

'I told her we'd phone back, make another appointment – soon.'

He stood, looking as if he was about to say something else but wasn't quite sure how.

'I don't want to worry you,' he said, as Mum looked towards him, 'but have you seen Kyra?'

'No,' said Mum, glancing at her watch. 'I thought she must have been out in the garden when Hannah fell. But she'd usually be in, demanding lunch by now. Have you looked in her room?'

'I've looked everywhere. She's not in her room or the garden,' Dad said, 'and her mobile's on her bed so there's no point phoning her.'

'Well, she's bound to be around somewhere,' Mum said. 'Kyra doesn't just wander off without telling us and she never goes anywhere without her phone.'

Hannah felt goose pimples prickling her skin and her throat tightened.

'We had a row,' she said, while she could still get the words out. 'I hit her.'

'What?' said Dad. 'Bloody hell, Hannah!'

'Not hard, I'm sure it wasn't hard, I just sort of pushed her away but she was crying. She ran out, just before I fell.'

'She'll be all right,' said Mum, as if trying to convince herself. 'She'll be around or maybe she's gone to one of her friends.'

But Dad had looked everywhere, he said, and none of Kyra's friends lived close enough to just call on. Mum knew that, not least because Kyra was always demanding lifts.

'There's a list of her friends' numbers in the kitchen drawer,' Mum said, standing up, 'I'll...'

'No, it's OK,' Dad said, 'I'll do it and I'll phone your mother as well.'

'No, don't start worrying, Mum. Kyra won't have gone there. It's too far.'

It wasn't really that far. Like most of Kyra's friends' houses, it didn't take long to get to Gran's by car, but on foot or by bus it'd take ages and anyway, Kyra didn't do buses. Hannah didn't think she'd know how. Mum was right, Kyra must be around somewhere. Nothing else bad could happen, it couldn't. Hannah stood up.

'I'll look outside. I'm fine,' she said, as Mum put her arm out to stop her, 'moving might do me good.'

Moving might well be doing her good but it wasn't easy. The pain in her right knee was the worst but she found she could just about manage if she didn't put her foot down flat. She checked the back garden first. She even checked the garden shed although she knew there was no way Kyra would be in there. Kyra hated the spiders and the cobwebs. She wouldn't so much as put her hand in there to drag her bike out, but Hannah looked anyway. The bike was there but no Kyra so Hannah walked down the side of the house, onto the drive, calling Kyra's name. Nothing.

Was it her fault? Had Kyra run off because of what she'd said, what she'd done? If it was any other twelve year old, you wouldn't think so. If it was any other twelve year old out in the middle of the day, you wouldn't even worry. But Kyra was such a kid, not what you'd call streetwise.

Hannah stopped at the end of the drive and looked both ways down the street. OK so what if Kyra hadn't gone anywhere at all? She might just be hiding somewhere. Deliberately freaking people out, trying to make sure she got her fair share of attention again. Oh God, she could really do without this. If Kyra was just mucking about, she'd kill her!

'Kyra!' she shouted again, as she hobbled back up the drive.

'It's all right,' her dad called back, appearing out of the garage clutching his mobile. 'Your gran's phoned. Kyra's turned up back there. She's a bit upset. Your gran's going to look after her. She'll probably keep her overnight again. Come on, come back inside, you've gone really pale.'

Mum was in the hall. She'd just put the house phone down.

'Was that Gran?' Hannah asked.

'No,' said Mum, 'that was the police. They need to talk to you again.'

'Why?' said Hannah, sitting on the stool next to the phone. 'What now?'

'I'm not sure. They said they needed to ask you a few more questions. I told them about the fall. I said you weren't feeling too good and they said it could wait till tomorrow morning.'

'I don't know why they're hassling Hannah,' Dad snapped. 'It's him they need to speak to.'

'They already have,' Mum said. 'I don't think his story checks out with Hannah's.'

'Oh, what a surprise,' said Dad. 'Like we ever expected him to admit it!'

Dad was right. Shane wasn't going to admit it, not even to himself. Shane wasn't exactly good at facing up to things at the best of times. He'd have convinced himself by now that she'd agreed or instigated it even. And if it came down to his word against hers, she knew who the cops would believe; she'd always known.

17

Lucy was standing by the window, her arms folded, her head tilted slightly to the left. Shane had known she'd come round. He'd thought about asking Dad to say he was still asleep or something but, when Lucy turned up, Dad was out. Besides there was no point putting it off so he'd let Lucy in and told her the basics.

'Oh my God,' Lucy was saying, 'it's crazy. I don't believe it. I don't believe she'd say something like that. What a cow! What a complete and total cow!'

His version had been very, very basic; just that Hannah had made an allegation and that he'd denied it. Lucy wouldn't be happy with that though. Any minute now, when the shock wore off, she'd start asking questions.

'Why?' she went on, almost immediately. 'Why the hell would Hannah say that? I don't get it. I mean you read about stuff like that. Girls stitching

173

blokes up to get their own back or something, but if it was some sort of mad revenge thing she'd have done it earlier when we first got together. What the hell's she playing at?'

'I dunno,' he mumbled.

'D'you want me to try and talk to her? Maybe I could—'

'No! Don't go near her, don't say nothing to anyone. This is serious, Luce!'

'Yeah, all right but—'

'I'm not supposed to talk about it or nothing. Not till it's all sorted out.'

'No, but everyone's gonna find out, aren't they? The cops'll have to check with people. I mean that should prove she's lying cos you left the party early, right? So all they need to do is check who you talked to, who you were with.'

'Yeah, I suppose.'

'So when exactly was all this supposed to have happened? You weren't with Hannah on her own or nothing, were you? You said you barely saw her at the party, didn't you?'

When he'd let Lucy in, he'd thought he'd be able to work round it somehow. That Dad might come back and tell Lucy to leave. Or maybe that he could miss out the main stuff, explain it in a way that would get Lucy on side. But he knew now that he couldn't. He was usually quite a good liar. Give or take a bit of blushing, he could wriggle his way out of most things, but not this. He knew the stress, the worry, was in his eyes, on his face. Lucy was looking at him as though every detail was written there in black letters.

'Shane?' she said.

He could feel tears building up, starting to trickle out to be used in evidence against him!

'Oh my God!' Lucy said again but the tone was different this time. 'Shane, you didn't! You couldn't!'

'It's not what you think,' he said, getting up, talking rapidly.

But Lucy didn't much care about little details like whether Hannah had consented or not. It didn't matter to her that he'd been wrongly accused of rape. The fact that he'd been anywhere near Hannah, under any circumstances, was bad enough for Lucy. He'd barely got the first couple of sentences out when she screamed. He moved towards her.

'Don't! Don't come near me,' she screeched, as Shane heard Dad's car pull up. 'How could you, how could you do that? I knew something had happened. I knew on Sunday! I could sense it. I knew it. God, I'm going to be sick!'

He heard the click of Dad's key in the door as Lucy pushed past him, her hand clamped over her mouth.

'Don't say nothing,' he heard himself pleading. 'Don't tell no one. Lucy, please!'

He wasn't even sure that she'd heard him as she rushed out and, even if she had, it wouldn't make any difference. She'd tell her mum, her dad, Jackie, Eden, Stacy, Clare, Mica, Liam, anyone who'd listen. Within an hour everyone would know.

18

Zak stood on the lawn with his dad, both of them admiring the bench. Zak had to admit they'd done a good job. He'd kept his promise and come straight home after his shift last night, mainly because he'd been completely knackered and his ribs were killing him. He hadn't mentioned his ribs to the boss, but the boss couldn't help but notice Zak's face.

'Jesus, Zak,' he'd said, 'you're going to frighten all the bloody customers! You look like a bloody zombie.'

Zombie or not, the boss had been too desperate for help to send him home and too busy to moan – much. Even though he was shattered when he got back, Zak had sat up for an hour with his dad last night, watching TV and having a couple of beers, which had killed off the pain a bit and helped him to sleep. Thankfully he hadn't heard any more freaky voices, no more signs of concussion or whatever it was.

He'd got up quite early too, by his standards, and without Dad shouting him. He'd come straight down to finish sanding and painting the bench, only stopping briefly to send a text to Hannah, although he'd known it was a waste of time. He'd sent one to Clare as well, which was just as pointless. Clare had answered but she hadn't been able to tell him much. She hadn't seen Hannah since Sunday. Hannah wasn't replying to messages and Clare hadn't wanted to go round hassling her again. So that was that. He was getting precisely nowhere.

'It looks good,' said Dad. 'We'll just have to hope it doesn't rain again before it dries. And thanks, thanks for helping.'

Zak turned away. He wished his dad wouldn't do that, wished he wouldn't sound so pathetically grateful. Dad had been just the same earlier on when Zak had done a bit of weeding between coats of bench paint.

'Good Lord, look at the time,' Dad said. 'It's almost half-past two, no wonder I'm hungry! Do you want some lunch?'

'Yeah, OK,' Zak said, even though he knew it would probably be something healthy like cheese salad on a wholemeal roll, without any mayo.

In the old days it had been Mum who was keen on the healthy food and Dad who'd make him bacon butties on Saturday morning or buy him burgers when they were out. But now that Dad was determined to turn into Mum, it was different.

When Dad went inside, Zak took his phone out of his pocket. He couldn't have missed any calls or messages but he checked anyway. He was right. There was nothing from Hannah and nothing more from Clare. He tried to convince himself that it was good news, that whatever had been kicking off at Hannah's yesterday had sorted itself out, but somehow he knew that wasn't true.

He stood for a moment, just staring at the phone. Either which way, he shouldn't have gone chasing around, getting himself beaten up. His dad and the boss could be right, he supposed. He might have anger-management issues but he wasn't going near any psychologists or counsellors. Shrinks just made things worse, or so Jed said.

The mere thought of all the prying and probing made him feel sick. So he stopped thinking, went into the kitchen, wiped off the paint he'd smeared on his phone, washed his hands and tried not to groan as he saw Dad piling salad between two slices of grainy bread. He was just putting the phone back in his pocket when it rang. It was Lee Broadhurst. Zak really didn't want to be bothered with Lee right now. He thought about ignoring it but, in the end, he couldn't resist answering just on the off chance that it could be something important.

'Uh, what?' he said as Lee gabbled something about a mate who'd been down the cop shop that morning and seen someone in there. 'Uh, are you sure?' Zak asked. 'Right, well, thanks.'

He wasn't sure why Lee was telling him or even *what* he was trying to tell him. Lee wasn't easy to understand at the best of times and he was so thick he was always getting stuff mixed up. Even if Lee was right, Zak knew it might not mean anything. He opened and closed his left hand, cracking the knuckles. This time he'd have to take it easy. He was in no state to go grabbing people by the throat, trying to shake information out of them, but there would be no harm in asking around.

'I've got to go out,' he told his dad.

'Where?'

'Just out.'

'What about your lunch?' Dad said, his voice loaded with disappointment.

'Stick it in the fridge, I'll have it later.'

19

Shane looked back towards the house as he walked down to the bottom of the garden. Mum would be asleep and he'd left Dad making a couple of calls, trying to reschedule his work. He leaned against the high fence, the barrier that shielded him from Mrs Yates next door, and took out a cigarette. He never usually smoked at home. His parents would go ballistic if they knew and Mrs Yates would surely tell them if she was out in her garden, if she smelled the smoke. She was always bloody nebbing and interfering, but what the hell? He needed a cigarette and being caught smoking was the least of his problems.

The flame from his lighter flickered in the slight breeze and his hand was shaking. He held his hand steady, tried again. This time it worked but it didn't really help. No amount of cigarettes was going to calm him down and they certainly weren't going to change anything.

'Shane!'

He automatically stubbed it out as he heard his dad's voice. It was crazy. He'd just been accused of rape and here he was, worried about being caught smoking!

'There's someone to see you,' Dad said as he walked towards him.

Oh, bollocks, Lucy was back or, even worse, the cops again.

'A young woman,' Dad said. 'She wouldn't say who she was or what she wanted but she wouldn't go away either. She's out the front. I hope she's not a flaming journalist. How do they get onto stuff so fast?'

Only she wasn't out the front and she wasn't a reporter. Eden was pushing the side gate open, storming towards them, or doing her best to storm, which wasn't easy with her killer heels puncturing the lawn. Lucy had obviously been blabbing already! News had got round, although why Eden should think it was any of her business, Shane wasn't sure.

'It's all right,' Shane said as his Dad looked from him to Eden, 'she's a friend.' Eden didn't look very friendly, admittedly. Her face was all flushed and she looked like she was about to explode.

'You shouldn't be talking to people,' Dad muttered.

Did Dad know who she was, had he guessed? Unlikely because Eden didn't look much like the tart Shane had described in his police interview. She was wearing a blue dress that hung below her knees, with a jacket draped over her shoulders, so apart from the killer heels she looked smart not slutty. Smart enough for Dad to mistake her for a local reporter. So had she been with her bloke? Was this the special grown-up look that she reserved for Mystery Man, the sophisticated look Jackie had droned on about?

'It's too late for that,' Shane insisted, as Eden approached. 'She already knows, I can tell. And if she knows, you can bet everybody knows.'

His dad looked as though he planned to stay around but with both Shane and Eden glaring at him, he shrugged and headed back to the house.

'What the bloody hell do you think you're playing at?' Eden hissed, as soon as his dad had left.

'Look,' Shane said, not really knowing why he was bothering to explain, 'I don't know what Lucy's told you but—'

'Lucy hasn't told me anything, I haven't even seen bloody Lucy.'

Hannah then, Hannah must have said something but surely Eden was one of the last people Hannah would talk to?

'And Hannah's lying,' he said, 'she knew what she was doing, I didn't—'

'I don't care what you did or what Hannah's saying. You're both pathetic,' Eden snapped. 'What I care about, Shane, is me.'

No surprise there then, but he still couldn't work out what she was on about so maybe they were talking at cross-purposes, maybe she didn't know at all!

'Why did you have to bring me into it?' she said, her voice getting ever louder.

'Huh?' said Shane.

Were they talking about the same thing or what?

'The cops!' Eden screamed. 'Why did you have to tell them about us, what we did?'

Shane didn't answer immediately. He couldn't. OK so they were obviously talking about the same thing, but he couldn't work out how Eden knew. It wasn't possible. Nobody knew what he'd told the cops apart from the people who'd been in the interview room. Although Hannah might know what he'd said, if the cops had reported back to her.

'So you've seen Hannah?' he said.

'No, I haven't seen Hannah and I don't bloody want to.'

'So—' Shane began.

'God, you really are thick, aren't you?' Eden said, her cat eyes narrowed and dangerous, her finger pointing at him, stabbing like a blade.

'The police,' Shane said, 'the police have been round checking my story?'

Not pleasant having the cops turn up, he knew that, but it wasn't like they were accusing Eden of anything criminal. And she surely wasn't the type to get embarrassed.

'Not officially, no,' she said. 'Stevie told me.'

'Who the hell's Stevie?' Shane asked.

But even as the words were coming out, he knew. It was starting to make some sort of sense. Stevie, Steven; that was the younger cop's name. PC Steven Smith, the cop who'd looked like he wanted to jump across the interview table and kill him the minute he'd admitted making out with Eden. The one who'd looked like he was going to throw up when Shane had confirmed Eden's full name and explained exactly what the making out had involved. That wasn't normal, no way! Why hadn't he seen it before? The cop was older than

Eden, sure, but not that much older, only five or six years maybe.

'He's your bloke,' Shane said, answering his own question. 'That bloody cop I talked to – he's your Mystery Man.'

'He was,' said Eden, 'but he probably isn't any more, thanks to you.'

'And he told you,' said Shane, 'he told you what I said?'

'Yeah and it wasn't exactly complimentary was it? "Total bitch" for starters, "slag who'd go with anyone", "tart", "devious lying cow", do I need to go on?'

Oh shit, he'd got so freaked in that interview, he'd said all that and more to Eden's bloke!

'He shouldn't have told you none of that,' Shane said. 'It's supposed to be confidential; he can't just go around telling everyone.'

'It's not all he told me,' said Eden, 'and I'm not just anyone. We've been together for nearly six months!'

'I don't get it,' said Shane. 'Why keep it secret, is he married or something?'

'No!'

'So why didn't you tell anyone? If I'd known who he was—'

'Like I was gonna admit I was going out with a cop, yeah? Just how many mates do you think I'd have left?'

She had a point. It wouldn't have done much for her image. The idea of Eden going anywhere near a cop was just mad. It was the last thing he'd ever have imagined and Smith just didn't seem her type, no way!

'I don't believe it,' he said. 'This is insane.'

'Maybe, but true,' said Eden, biting her bottom lip as she paused. 'I really liked him. It was different, it was really going somewhere.'

'It didn't look that way on Saturday night when you had your hand down my jeans!'

Shane barely had time to wish the words back in his mouth when Eden's right hand lashed out and belted him across the face.

'Nothing happened on Saturday night,' Eden yelled, as he rubbed his stinging cheek. 'You got that? I told Stevie what I told Hannah. You were droning on about your pathetic little love life. We went upstairs to talk. You were drunk. You tried to shove your hand up my skirt.'

'No, you know that's not true, you can't say that.'

'I can and I did,' said Eden. 'I pushed you away then Hannah came in, then you left. That's what happened, OK? Oh, and I gave Hannah that daft story because I felt sorry for you! Didn't want her to know what a sleazy, cheating git you really are!'

'No!' Shane said. 'You can't do that, you can't say that. It makes me look like a total liar.'

'You are a liar, Shane. All that stuff you said about me!'

'No, you know what happened. You know you came onto me. You know exactly what happened. I mean why? Why come onto me in the first place if you were so keen on your cop?'

But he knew the answer. It was pure boredom, Eden having a bit of fun. No one was supposed to ever find out. Eden was smiling at him now.

'I don't know what you were on, on Saturday night, Shane,' Eden said, her voice oozing false sweetness, 'but it's sure affected your memory.'

Shane didn't know what Hannah believed to be true, but it was clear enough what was going on with Eden. She was lying and they both knew it. She was totally, totally stitching him up just so her bloody bloke wouldn't dump her. Shane accepted that he might, just might, have misread some of the signals with Hannah on Saturday night but not with Eden, no way.

'You've got to tell him the truth,' he said, hearing his voice rising to a wail.

'No chance! It was supposed to be a laugh, Shane, and you've turned it into a frickin' nightmare.'

There it was, an admission, but what good would it do him?

'I think Stevie's starting to believe me,' Eden said. 'I think I can just about hold this together and that's exactly what I'm gonna do. I'll make a formal statement and go to court if I have to, whatever it takes.'

'You can't,' Shane said, 'you can't lie to a court.'

Oh God, he sounded so weak, so desperate, so pathetic.

'I can and I will. I'll tell as many lies as I have to. Just watch.'

'But if they don't believe me about you, they won't believe me about Hannah.'

'Tough,' said Eden, 'like I care.'

'Eden,' he said, grabbing her arm as she turned to walk away, 'this isn't a game. I could go to jail if they don't believe me!'

'Get off me!' she said, tearing at his hand with her nails as she pulled away. 'You shouldn't have dragged me into this, Shane! It's your own stupid fault. And now it's your word against mine and Hannah's. Do the maths!'

Shane sank down onto the grass as he watched her walk away. If this was a film or something, he'd have recorded her lies, he'd have some proof, but he hadn't and he didn't. He hadn't kept her texts and even if he had they'd be no use, they were too vague. She'd been careful. And, of course, there were no witnesses. So now he had two girls making out like he was some sleazy predator. He was screwed, totally screwed.

20

Zak swung into the supermarket car park, which was crowded for late on a Wednesday afternoon. He pulled up in the first space he saw, his car drawing everyone's attention as usual. Zak pushed open the door, got out and almost bumped into an elderly man who was just getting into his BMW in the next space. The man tutted at him but Zak didn't take any notice. His eyes were fixed on the group over by one of the trolley bays.

He'd phoned Clare before setting off but he hadn't really needed to check. He'd sort of known where they'd all be. Kids who were still at school treated the supermarket car park like a youth club. There were at least a dozen or so clustered round now. Most of them Zak recognised though he didn't know all their names. Some like Clare, Jackie and Liam were in their work clothes, either on a break or bunking off, while others like Lucy were obviously just lured by text messages, picking up the news. Although Zak wasn't sure what the latest news would turn out to be. Clare had seemed confused when he'd spoken to her and what Lee had said didn't exactly make sense either.

'Blimey,' said Clare as he approached, 'what's happened to your face?'

'Nothing. Has Shane been arrested? Is it something to do with Hannah?'

'Well yeah, sort of, some of it,' said Clare, her eyes looking everywhere but at him. 'Lucy knows. She's seen him.'

Zak turned to look at Lucy. He couldn't get a good view because Jackie had her arms wrapped round her but he could see that Lucy's face looked almost as bad as his own. It wasn't mangled like his but it was all red, puffy and swollen-eyed. She was sniffing and sobbing almost like she was choking. He obviously wasn't going to get much from Lucy so he turned to Clare again, who looked down at the tarmac.

'What?' Zak said. 'Just tell me.'

'According to Lucy, Shane reckons he went back to Hannah's on Saturday night and had sex with her,' one of the lads announced, 'and now Hannah's like making out that he raped her.'

A scream made everyone look towards Lucy as she pulled away from Jackie and ran off.

'Watch out!' someone yelled as Lucy ran right in front of a bright-pink car.

Luckily it was only crawling because Lucy didn't stop. She didn't respond to the shout or the blare of the horn or screech of the brakes. It was like she just hadn't noticed.

'I'll go,' said Clare, as Jackie was about to set off after her.

Zak watched while Jackie held Clare back for a moment, whispering something to her. His eyes followed Clare as she set off, caught up with Lucy by the far wall and put her arms round her, like Jackie had done. Everyone had started talking, but above it all Zak could hear the thud of his own heart. Bloody Shane, the beat seemed to be tapping out. Shane had— Zak couldn't bring himself even to think the word. He tried to focus, to tune into the talk going on around him but he felt dizzy and all he could hear were the words: Shane and Hannah, Hannah and Shane.

'I'll kill him,' he muttered, the words disappearing down into his throat, rather than out for everyone to hear, 'I'll kill the bastard.'

'You all right, mate?' someone said, as Zak's

mutter turned into a sort of growl.

Zak blinked. He didn't recognise the speaker straight away but then realised it was Liam, the kid he'd been round to see on Sunday when he'd been on the trail of the stuff Jed and Lee had nicked.

'Yeah, I'm fine,' he said, shaking his head at the same time, forcing himself to listen, to make out sentences from the general buzz of noise.

'I know Hannah's a bit of a snotty cow,' Jackie was saying, 'but she wouldn't just lie, not about something like that.'

'And Shane wouldn't rape no one, no way,' said Liam. 'It's obvious what happened.'

'Is it?' said Jackie.

'Oh, come on!' said Liam. 'She's been trying to get back with—'

He stopped, looked at Zak.

'Nothing, it don't matter,' Liam said. 'I just know Shane wouldn't do nothing like that.'

'Yeah, well that's not what Eden said,' Jackie snarled. 'He came onto her at the party too! She had to bloody fight him off, she said. Our Shane's not as sweet and innocent as he likes to make out.'

'That's bollocks,' another girl said.

'You sayin' I'm lying, Stace?' Jackie said. 'You callin' our Eden a liar?'

'No,' said Stacy, stepping back, 'I'm sayin' we don't know the full story, that's all. We don't know what went on with Shane and Hannah. We weren't there!'

'Yeah, but if it's true,' Jackie said, 'what he did to Hannah, I mean it's like totally wrong, innit? And I know who I believe!'

'Yeah,' said Stacy, 'but there's no point taking sides, stirring it all up, believing one of them or the other. Not till we know a bit more.'

The sensible, rational part of Zak thought she was probably right but she was way too late. People had already taken sides. Comments were bouncing around with half a dozen people all yelling at once now, really loud, which was totally doing his head in.

'Oh shit,' he heard Jackie shriek, her voice rising above the rest, 'there's the bloody manager. I gotta go. Somebody get Clare, she's due back too.'

Zak set off across the car park, before anyone else could move. Partly to get Clare but mainly because he didn't want to hear everyone going on about it any more; he couldn't trust himself not to lash out at the next person who said something bad about Hannah. Clare was heading back anyway and there was no sign of Lucy.

'Lucy's gone home,' Clare said, as they met in the middle of the car park. 'She said she'll be OK but I'm not so sure. She's in a right state. I mean she didn't say anything to me but if Jackie's right . . .'

'Right about what? I mean I saw Jackie whisper something to you.'

'Nothing, it's nothing,' Clare said. 'I just can't believe any of this is happening. What a mess, what a bloody stupid mess!'

'You could say that.'

'Mica reckons there's stuff online already, on all the network sites,' Clare said. 'I don't know how it's got round so fast.'

'Not hard to work out,' said Zak, looking back to what was left of the group.

Some were still arguing, shouting loud enough for half the town to hear. A couple were on their mobiles and some girl, whose name he didn't know, was tapping away at her Blackberry.

'It's just mad,' said Clare, 'the way they're all mouthing off, taking sides when no one really knows what went on.'

'That's what that Stacy girl was sayin' but I think we know enough,' Zak said.

'Zak,' Clare said, lightly touching his arm as he turned to leave, 'don't . . .'

She paused, like she was scared of him. Was that really the message he gave off; that even girls had to be scared of him? Was that why Hannah had dumped him, was it all his own fault? If he'd stopped getting so wasted, stopped hanging round with Jed, like Hannah wanted, would they still be together? Could he have stopped this happening?

'What?' he said, as calmly as he could manage, while the questions still screamed at him.

'Don't do anything stupid,' she said, 'don't get involved.'

He nodded at her. He even managed a sort of smile, but he wasn't sure he could do what she said because he was already involved and nothing was going to change that.

21

Hannah looked from her phone to the laptop screen, her throat dry, her eyes blurred with tears. Why had she done it, why had she switched her phone on again? That's right, she was going to send a text to Kyra, apologising for hitting her, before she remembered Kyra didn't have her phone with her anyway.

Besides, all thoughts of Kyra had gone out of her head when she'd seen the messages, dozens of them, some from people she barely knew, calling her a lying slag and worse. Even the supportive ones made her want to throw up. There'd been a load of gush from Jackie, oozing false sympathy, saying what a total bastard Shane was. Why hadn't she just switched off, right then, stopped reading them? But she couldn't, she'd read on, sorting out her friends from her enemies. She'd even thought about replying to Clare but then another one had popped up from someone telling her not to look online.

Networking had been the last thing on her mind but the warning had made her look. She couldn't help herself. Oh, God, how could they write things like that? How had it spread so fast, how had it even started? She didn't really need to ask. Lucy, it was obviously Lucy who'd started it. Most people were taking sides, slagging off either her or Shane, but Lucy had got her talons into both of them.

It barely seemed possible that this was the same Lucy she'd been friends with since infants, the girl she'd played in the Wendy house with, the one she'd giggled her way through primary school with. They'd both fancied Shane when they were younger, all the girls did, but it had been innocent back then, something to laugh and joke about. And that's the way it had stayed until she was in Year Ten when the lads in the year above had started growing up, taking an interest – when Shane had chosen her.

Sure Lucy hadn't been exactly pleased but she'd seemed OK with it. She'd gone out with Liam for a while then Ash, from the Lower Sixth, but all the time Lucy had been watching, waiting for a chance, going with Shane behind her bloody back for weeks before that school trip when Jackie had been sent to spell it out for her.

'Listen, babes, someone's gotta tell you and it may as well be me. You're dumped, Hannah. Shane's with Lucy now.'

And now Lucy had turned on both of them, spreading it everywhere. More messages and comments springing up like poisonous toadstools as Hannah watched. It felt as if it wasn't ever going to stop, like every detail of her life was suddenly public property. Like she didn't already feel bad enough, like people had to go out of their way to make it all worse.

22

Shane lay awake staring at the red numbers slowly changing on his clock. 02:04, 02:05. Thursday morning already and it was impossible to sleep. He hadn't even gone to bed till midnight because he'd been waiting to hear from the police. He was sure they'd have talked to Hannah again, sure that Eden would have given a statement, sure that they'd get back to him, but they hadn't and the waiting was killing him.

They were about the only bloody people who hadn't been in touch. He'd been bombarded by texts and phone calls. Mostly the texts were from people who weren't brave enough to actually speak to him; people he'd thought were his mates. OK so there'd been one or two sympathetic texts but the rest... God it made him want to puke.

He looked at the clock again, 02:07. Some of the texts had told him to look on Facebook and stuff but he hadn't dared and, in the end, he'd switched the phone off. He'd sat doing nothing except watching his dad pacing round the house. He'd told Dad all about Eden so he had got onto the solicitor, who'd made reassuring noises, but it was hopeless. They all knew it was hopeless, how bad it looked.

'Just tell the truth, Shane,' Mum had said when she'd appeared, briefly, looking terrible, 'just keep telling the truth, that's all you can do. No one who knows you could believe what Hannah's saying.'

Oh, but they did. He switched on his phone. He looked at the new messages and some of the old ones, making himself feel sick again, wondering why he was doing it. Idiots like Jackie he could understand, especially as Eden had obviously got to her, spreading her venom, but Ravi! How could Ravi write stuff like that?

02:13. He dropped the phone as he heard a sharp crack, then another and another. The sound of breaking glass! The windows, somebody was smashing the windows. Bloody hell! He leaped up, pulled open the curtains and looked out onto the street. He couldn't see anything but he thought he heard footsteps running away.

He picked up a pair of grubby jogging bottoms from the floor and wriggled into them as he headed for the bedroom door. He wasn't sure that his parents would have heard from their bedroom at the back but, when he opened the door, the landing light was already on and his dad was near the top of the stairs. Shane followed him down and into the lounge. Dad switched on the light. The curtains were closed. They looked strangely undisturbed. There was no broken glass, no bricks lying on the carpet, but he couldn't have imagined it. Dad had obviously heard it too.

'Be careful,' Shane said as his dad pulled back the curtains.

The glass was still in place. The windows were fine with not so much as a crack.

'It definitely came from the front,' Shane said.

They checked the small dining room on the other side and the downstairs loo next to the door but there was nothing, no sign of any disturbance. They couldn't both have dreamed it though!

'Don't go out,' Shane said when his dad unfastened the chain on the front door and put on a jacket over his pyjamas.

'It might be the garage windows,' Dad said.

'So leave them, leave it till tomorrow.'

But his dad wasn't listening. He was opening the front door and the nutters who did it might still be hanging around! Shane had thought he'd heard someone running off but he could have been wrong. You saw stuff like that on the news; people who went out trying to protect their cars or their property getting beaten up or stabbed. Shane grabbed his trainers from the rack by the door and slipped them on.

'Dad,' he said, following him out, 'just call the cops.'

'We don't know anything's happened yet,' said his dad, standing on the path, looking right towards the garage windows, which were fine. Shane looked left over the low dividing fence and saw glass on the small front lawn.

'It's Mrs Yates's,' said Shane, putting his hand on the fence and vaulting over. His dad walked round, out of their gate and back through Mrs Yates's, looking up and down the street at the same time.

'Can't see anyone,' he said.

'No sign of Mrs Yates either,' said Shane. 'I think she's slept through it.'

Hard to believe, as all the lounge windows and her cloakroom windows to the right of the door were smashed, but then she was pretty deaf and he doubted if she wore her hearing aids in bed.

'We can't leave it like that,' his dad said. 'I'll have to board them up, sweep up the worst of the glass. You'd better ring the bell, Shane, while I get dressed and get some stuff from the garage. We need to clear away the glass inside too, in case she hurts herself, and anyway we'd better tell her what's going on before she gets scared. She's bound to hear the hammering.'

Shane wasn't sure about that. He rang the bell half a dozen times while his dad passed sheets of hardboard, a tool box and a sweeping brush over the fence but there was still no response. What if she *had* heard the breaking glass, got up in a hurry and fallen or something? She wasn't exactly steady on her feet at the best of times. Shane peered through the letterbox but it was dark inside her hallway and he couldn't see. She could be lying there at the bottom of the stairs. They really needed to phone the cops and an ambulance. His dad came out again, dressed this time.

'You can stop ringing,' Dad said. 'She'll be down in a minute. I phoned her. She has a phone next to the bed. I've told her to be careful of the glass and to put some shoes on.'

Shane started sweeping up some of the glass.

'What sort of person would do something like this to an old lady?' his dad was muttering as he opened up his tool box. 'Drunks probably, or kids,' he added, answering his own question, but Shane wasn't so sure.

He was going to say something when the door opened and Mrs Yates appeared, wrapped in a pink, fluffy dressing gown. Shane noticed she was shaking and who could blame her? He also noticed that she'd put shoes on like Dad said. She'd put her glasses on too and her hearing aids in but not her false teeth so her face looked all sort of collapsed, older and sadder than ever.

'Oh, my goodness,' she said, standing on the doorstep. 'Nowhere's safe any more not even your own home. It's a good job you heard them. They were probably going to break in. You hear such a lot about these things. I could have been murdered!'

Shane could hear the wheezing of her chest as she tried to breathe more deeply.

'I don't think,' Shane said slowly, 'I don't think it was meant for you.'

His dad looked up.

'Well, it's obvious,' Shane said. 'Some idiot got

the wrong house. It was meant for us, it was meant for me!'

'I'd already thought of that,' his dad said, 'but we don't know, we can't be sure.'

His dad might not be sure but *he* was. And this was only the start. He'd been found guilty before he got anywhere near a court.

'I'm sorry,' Shane said to Mrs Yates as she looked from him to his dad, totally bemused, 'this is my fault.'

'Is it something to do with the police coming round this morning, dear?' she asked, her words coming out in short bursts.

Shane nodded. No way could he tell Mrs Yates exactly what it was about, although she was sure to find out soon enough.

'And that girl you were talking to in the garden?' she added.

'What?' Shane said.

'I was weeding my borders,' Mrs Yates said, 'I shouldn't because it's bad for my back. And my doctor's always telling me to take it easy, since I had that last do with my heart. But you know me. I like to stay as active as I can.'

She was weeding her borders! She was probably right up against the fence. Mrs Yates's ears weren't too good but the aids made a big difference and Eden hadn't exactly been whispering. Mrs Yates could have heard. She could be the witness he needed, at least to get the Eden problem out of the way.

'What did you hear?' he asked, at the same time as all the thoughts, the hopes were tumbling into his head.

'Only snatches, dear,' she said. 'And I didn't really understand most of it, but it was obvious the girl was trying to get you into trouble.'

'Why didn't you say?' said Shane. 'Why didn't you tell me you'd heard?'

'Well, I thought about it but I didn't know how important it was and I didn't like to interfere.'

For the first time in his life he'd wanted his neighbour to interfere and she hadn't!

'So what exactly did you hear?' said Dad.

Shane was willing her to speak faster but the words were still coming out incredibly slowly, breathlessly.

'Oh dear, I can't remember all the details. My memory's hopeless these days. But the things she was saying – and I remember thinking, that can't be right, that doesn't sound like my Shane.'

It wasn't enough. She didn't remember enough, not enough to make a difference.

'And she didn't sound at all nice,' Mrs Yates, added. 'I mean she said she was going to lie in court and I thought, *Well that's just not right, is it?*'

That was it. That would do! Shane wanted to hug her but he thought it best not to, not least because he might actually squeeze the life out of her.

'And you'd tell the police?' he asked. 'You'd tell them what you heard?'

Mrs Yates yawned and put her hand up to her mouth.

'Sorry,' she said. 'I'm exhausted. But yes, I'll tell them, if it would help.'

Oh yes, it would help. It would help but would it be enough? If only there'd been a convenient witness on Saturday night at Hannah's. But there wasn't. It was just the two of them. So it was back to the main problem – his word against Hannah's.

23

Hannah sat on the edge of her chair, her hands clasped, resting on her legs. The cops had seemed sympathetic enough when they'd phoned, asking whether she was well enough to be interviewed again. When they'd heard how badly her knee had swelled, they'd offered to come round to save her the trouble of going to the station, but why did they need to talk to her at all? What else was she supposed to say?

PC Kate Campbell had calmly told them the results of the medical. There was no pregnancy, no infection and, she'd added, hesitantly, no sign of damage or violent struggle. In the same calm voice, PC Campbell had gone on to ask her about her fall, about how she was feeling, while Mum made tea and Dad grumbled to PC Smith about the lack of anything being done. But now everyone had sat down. The room had gone quiet and both cops were looking slightly uncomfortable, as if they didn't know where to begin.

'I'm afraid,' PC Campbell said, making Hannah clench her hands tighter, 'that we need you to clarify a few points. Shane insists that what happened on Saturday night was consensual. Do you understand what that means?'

'Yeah,' Hannah snapped, 'it means I agreed, but I didn't. I kept saying no, I tried to push him away, I told you!'

'And there couldn't have been any doubt?'

'No!'

'Shane also told us that your previous relationship had involved—'

'OK,' Hannah said, looking at her parents, knowing what PC Campbell was going to say. 'It's true. We'd had sex. So what? We'd been together a year. It's not like I sleep around. It was only Shane, he's the only one. I loved him!'

She heard her dad gasp like he'd never thought about it, never considered that she was growing up.

'It doesn't change what happened,' Dad said, standing up. 'It doesn't matter what happened before – it wouldn't matter if she was bloody married to him – she said no! That should be clear enough for anybody.'

'I understand what you're saying,' PC Campbell said, 'but the fact that Hannah lied about some things, that there was no actual violence involved, that she took so long to report it, all weakens the case.'

'You made me report it all! You told me to tell you everything,' Hannah said. 'You convinced me it would be all right! You can't just change your mind now.'

'I know,' said Campbell, 'and it's always right to report these things. We like to bring prosecutions whenever we can. But there are still some things we need to get clear first, like the text.'

'What text?' Mum said.

'Shane says Hannah sent him a text on Sunday afternoon, is that right?' Campbell said, looking straight at her.

Hannah nodded.

'And what did it say?'

'Just that we needed to talk,' she said, so quietly that she barely heard it herself.

The next questions screamed in her head even before anyone had a chance to ask them. Why had she done it, how could she have been so totally, totally stupid?

'I was confused,' she continued. 'I was still

hungover, I was trying to get my head straight. I didn't know what to do. I don't know why I sent it. It was stupid, I know that now.'

'He says he didn't reply, is that right?' Campbell asked.

'Yes,' said Hannah, 'I mean no, he didn't answer. I know how it looks but it wouldn't have made any difference to anything.'

'He thinks it might,' said Campbell. 'He's saying that you made the claim to get back at him. You agreed to intercourse but you were angry that he wasn't going to restart your relationship so—'

'No! I wouldn't do that. I wasn't lying. I told him no. I didn't want to, I didn't! I wasn't even going to tell anybody but I just kept thinking about it, thinking about what he'd done and then it all came out and you made me tell you. All of you! You said it was the right thing to do! And now you don't believe me.'

Her mum came over, wrapped her arms round her as she started to cry.

'It was,' Mum said. 'It is. And she's telling the truth,' she added, clearly talking to the police officers. 'I know Hannah and she's telling the truth.'

Campbell said something. Hannah couldn't quite make out the words but her dad's response came through loud and very clear.

'Are you telling me that you definitely can't prosecute? He's going to get away with this?'

'That's not up to us,' Campbell said, 'we just present the evidence to the Crown Prosecution Service but I'm not sure we've even got enough solid evidence to put forward a case. I'm sorry, I'm really sorry, I know how you must feel but it's so difficult.'

'This is why they get away with it,' Dad yelled. 'This is why some women don't report it. Have you seen the bloody state Hannah's in? What more evidence do you need?'

'Well,' said Campbell, slowly, drawing the word out, 'another girl's told us about a lesser incident with Shane on the night of the party, which might help to support Hannah's case.'

'What?' said Hannah, looking up, wiping her eyes with her hands. 'Who?'

'I can't say very much, at the moment,' Campbell said, 'but she said you saw her and Shane together.'

'Oh, Eden!' said Hannah.

What did they mean by an incident? Had Eden claimed Shane was trying to assault her or something? Was that possible, could Shane have been high on something that had made him act out of

214

character with both of them? But then on Saturday night Eden had sworn nothing had happened, her and Shane were just talking, she'd said. So what had made her change her mind? Whatever the reason, it was probably something devious and she didn't need Eden's help.

'Eden's a liar,' she said. 'I don't know what went on with her and Shane but you can't believe a word she says.'

The other cop, PC Smith, who'd said absolutely nothing, shuffled on his seat, glared at her then suddenly got up and walked out.

'What the hell's going on?' said Dad.

'Er, I'm not sure,' said Campbell, 'he's been a bit – he's not been feeling well.'

She stood up.

'I need to report back, consolidate all the evidence then I'll be in touch again, all right?'

Hannah shook her head. She didn't want to go ahead with this. She never really had, but it was too late. If she tried to pull back now it would look like she'd been lying all along. Everyone at school, everyone who knew her, would think she'd lied! And Dad was right, in a way, if people didn't report these things, it'd keep on happening, hidden away as if it didn't matter.

As her parents showed PC Campbell out, Hannah got up and stared out of the window. It didn't seem possible that everything still looked the same as it had always done. On the outside nothing had changed, but on the inside everything had.

24

Zak stormed through the house to the kitchen where his dad was chopping vegetables.

'You're early,' Dad said.

'Boss let me go just after two,' Zak said, dragging a chair from under the table and sitting down. 'I was struggling a bit anyway with my rib and stuff, then the bloody cops turned up at work, wanting to talk to me. And, like, all the customers are staring, wondering what's going on. Anyway you might get a call. They might want to check out my story.'

'Why, what's happened now?'

'Nothing,' said Zak, 'I haven't done nothing. Some old woman's windows got smashed in the early hours of this morning and they reckoned it might have been me.'

'Why you? You were home last night.'

'That's what I told 'em. But it's sort of complicated. It's not really about the old woman.'

'So what is it about?'

'It's a long story. It's sort of to do with another case.'

'That's all right, I'm listening.'

His dad had finished chopping vegetables, made them into a pasta sauce, divided it into three smaller dishes for freezing, like his mum used to do, and had done all the clearing up by the time Zak had given him the story, stretching back to the day he first met Hannah.

'So they think the bricks were meant for this Shane?' Dad said, shaking his head as if he just didn't get the modern world at all, which he probably didn't.

'Yeah and they might be right.'

'But it was definitely nothing to do with you?'

'No!'

In a way he wished it was. He'd thought about it. He'd spent all last night lying awake, thinking about Hannah and Shane. Knowing the old Zak would have done something about it, knowing that something, somehow, had started to change.

'No,' he said, again. 'If it was me I'd have got the right bloody house.'

25

Hannah quickly closed down her laptop when she heard the knock on the bedroom door. It had to be Dad. Only Dad ever knocked.

'Yeah,' she said.

He opened the door but didn't come in.

'I've got to go round to your gran's,' Dad said. 'Kyra's had a bit of an accident.'

'Accident?' said Hannah, standing up. 'What sort of accident, is she all right?'

It didn't seem possible that anything else bad could have happened; that life could just keep on getting worse.

'She's OK. I don't think it's serious. She fell off a swing in the park, apparently. But I shouldn't leave your gran to cope with everything and your mum's had to pop into work for an hour. So will you be all right?'

'Yeah, but I want to come with you.'

'Well, if you're sure.'

She was sure, partly because she wanted to see whether Kyra was all right and partly because it would stop her obsessively looking at networking sites. More and more posts had been appearing all through the afternoon and into the early evening, as people finished work and raced home to their computers to spread all the dirt!

As they headed to Gran's, she thought about telling Dad. She even opened her mouth once or twice but she couldn't do it. She couldn't find the words to tell him how bad it had got, how venomous people were being, not just about her and Shane either. Bloody Jackie had even started a rumour that Lucy was pregnant! It couldn't be true. Lucy wouldn't be so stupid. But if it was, if Lucy was pregnant now? How would she feel, what on earth would she do?

Hannah wasn't even sure why she cared but part of her did. She didn't care as much about Jackie's other bit of news, about Eden's love life, but it was well weird. It was so bizarre that Hannah would never, ever have believed it if she hadn't seen PC Smith's reaction earlier. Eden and a cop! It had set off loads of comments online. Not quite enough to draw attention away from her though, especially as it was all hopelessly connected.

What was it about the bloody internet, what made people like Jackie think it was fine to broadcast everyone's private lives? With any luck Eden would kill her when she saw what she'd written. Hannah shook her head. She couldn't bear to keep thinking about it all, so she asked Dad about Kyra instead.

'I've told you all I know,' he said. 'Kyra went out to the park to meet up with some of her ballet friends and came back in "a bit of a state", as Gran put it. It honestly doesn't sound like much.'

By the time they got there, Gran had obviously tried to clean Kyra up but she didn't look much like Kyra at all. She looked more like Zak after one of his nights out with Jed! Her hair was hanging loose and grubby. Her legs had faint smears of mud, her bottom lip was split and she still had a blood-soaked tissue clamped to her nose.

'Oh God, what's happened to you?' said Hannah, automatically going over and giving her a hug, something she hadn't done for months, maybe even years.

'She said she fell off a swing,' Gran said, looking towards Dad, 'but Bibi's mother's just phoned and Bibi said Kyra got in a fight.'

A fight, Kyra, no way! Kyra didn't do fighting – except with her sometimes.

'Is this true?' Dad asked.

'Yes,' said Kyra, her chin tilted in a defiant pose, which didn't really suit her.

'Who?' said Gran. 'Why? Were you being bullied or something?'

'Some older girls,' Kyra announced, almost proudly, 'two of them. Year Nines.'

'Which girls,' said Dad, 'what are their names?'

'Don't know their names,' said Kyra, though she probably did, 'and they didn't start the fight, I did!'

'Why?' said Dad. 'This isn't like you, Kyra.'

No, it wasn't, which is why Hannah knew the reason even before Kyra said it. She knew the comments had gone beyond cyberspace and were spreading out in the park, on the street.

'They were saying stuff,' Kyra said, 'really bad stuff about Hannah, so I thumped them.'

26

Shane looked up as his mum came in to his room, waving a bit of paper.

'I don't believe this,' she said. 'Another flaming note shoved though the letterbox and some stuff scrawled on the front gate in red graffiti. I don't know whether it's the same person or different ones each time but who's to say it won't be bricks again tonight?'

She dropped the note on his bed and stood by the window, staring out, tapping her fingers on the windowsill. Shane didn't touch the paper. He didn't need to read it. He could read crap like that on his mobile any time and online if he could be bothered to look, which so far he couldn't.

'I'm thinking,' Mum said, 'that we ought to go somewhere, go to a hotel or something for a while.'

'Maybe,' he said. 'But what about Mrs Yates, I mean what if they get the wrong house again?

We can't leave her stuck here on her own. I mean, she's terrified it's gonna happen again.'

'I know,' said Mum. 'Maybe we can persuade her to come with us or stay with that friend of hers, Moira, for a day or two. I ought to go over and see her anyway. Your dad said she was really shaken up. I've just got a couple of things I need to do first then I'll pop round.'

'I'll go,' said Shane, standing up.

'All right,' said Mum, 'tell her I'll be round in twenty minutes or so.'

Mum was looking at him like she couldn't believe he'd actually volunteered to go round there. He couldn't believe it either. Normally Mrs Yates would be the last person he'd want to see but she'd done him a massive, massive favour by talking to the police this afternoon. The Eden factor was more or less wiped out, gone, sorted.

He sighed as he left the bedroom. It wasn't just about Eden though. It was weird but he was sort of worried about Mrs Yates too. She'd looked so pale by the time him and Dad had put the new windows in and her breathing had been all kind of heavy, even more wheezy than usual. It had suddenly hit him just how old she was and how a shock like this would get to her.

Somehow instead of thinking how she bored him to death and drove him nuts, he'd started thinking about how nice she'd always been to him, the way she'd given him money for birthdays and Christmas. The way she always asked how he was doing at school and stuff, like she was really interested, really cared.

His phone rang as he headed downstairs so he reached into his pocket and switched it off. It would only be more of the same. Hate mail or sympathy, it hardly mattered. Eden might be out of the way but the main problem wasn't ever going to go away, whatever the police or the bloody Crown Prosecution Service decided.

Everyone knew about it. Even the school had found out. Holidays or not, the head had been on the phone to Dad saying they'd need to come in before the start of term to 'discuss Shane's future'. Which meant he didn't have a future, not at this school anyway. It meant they didn't want him back, that he was supposed to find somewhere else to finish his A levels. He bet Hannah would be back there though because poor Hannah was the victim, wasn't she? Oh yes, girls always were!

He slumped on the bottom stair feeling suddenly exhausted, like he could barely be bothered to breathe. In less than a week his life had fallen apart and rearranged itself into a totally different life. A life that didn't seem to belong to him at all – the sort of life you read about in the papers or watched being played out on daytime chat shows. If only he'd answered Hannah's text on Sunday afternoon maybe none of this would have happened. But then if he was going down the 'if only' route the starting point wasn't Sunday afternoon at all; it was the early hours of Sunday morning.

His head dropped down between his hands. He should never have gone round there. He knew that now. It all seemed so bloody obvious. But Hannah had sounded so frightened, so desperate. The way she'd clung to him when he'd turned up, the way she'd held onto him when he'd tried to get her onto her bed. Was it all part of her plan? Had she meant to set him up?

If so, he'd fallen right into the trap. He'd promised to help her, he'd told her it would all be all right. Then she'd kissed him on his cheek, on his lips and he'd known it was wrong, he'd known he shouldn't! But her tongue had slid into his mouth and she'd touched him so he could hardly bloody think straight.

Sure there'd been muttered words about Lucy and about Eden. Even the word 'no' had figured somewhere. But Hannah was just saying it wasn't right cos of Lucy and stuff. That's what she'd meant. She'd meant it wasn't nice, it wasn't right, it wasn't fair, not that she didn't bloody want to. She hadn't tried to stop him, she hadn't!

He pulled himself up, unlocked the front door and kicked it open.

'Where are you going?'

Dad's voice made Shane jump.

He swung round to see Dad standing in the lounge doorway.

'Just next door, Mum wants me to check on Mrs Yates.'

'Good idea,' said Dad, 'I was going to look in on her again myself. Take this,' he added, fishing in his trouser pocket, bringing out a key, 'in case she doesn't answer. She said she was going to have a lie down and gave me her spare key in case there were any more emergencies.'

Shane took the key but he didn't use it. It seemed wrong somehow just walking into Mrs Yates's house, so he rang the bell and waited when she didn't answer. She was a bit slow at the best of times, so it would take her a while to get to the door. He rang again. Still no answer but rather than use the key he went round the back. The sitting-room curtains were open so he looked in, standing back slightly so he didn't scare her. The last thing she needed right now was a face at her window. There was no sign of her so he moved in a bit closer, which is when he saw the empty chair and the figure slumped on the floor.

'Oh my God,' he said, dropping the key, which was still in his hand, and getting out his phone.

Emergency services first, trying to stay calm, trying to give the address, the important facts. Then he phoned Dad. It was quicker to phone than rush back to the house. By the time he'd picked up the key and got round to the front, his parents were there. He handed the key to Dad and followed his parents inside. She'd be all right. Mrs Yates would be OK. It was just a fall.

His mum was already crouched down by her.

'Don't touch her,' said Dad. 'I don't think we should touch her, we should wait for the paramedics.'

'I think it might be too late,' said Mum, her face crumpling.

No, *she was wrong. She had to be wrong.*

27

Shane stood at the hotel window on Friday morning, staring out over the city. They'd arrived at about three in the morning, after they'd been to the hospital. They'd got home and realised that they couldn't stay there because someone had been busy smashing up their bloody windows while they'd been away. Shane had been completely knackered, wiped out, but he hadn't slept. He hadn't even bothered lying down on the bed. He'd just sat in a chair, thinking and crying, reading texts including that new one, that awful one from Jackie about Lucy that set him off crying again.

Turning round, he headed across the room as he heard the sharp knock on the door. His dad came in, looked about vacantly then sat on the end of the bed.

'I've booked us in for another couple of nights,' Dad said.

Shane nodded. He didn't much care where they stayed, as long as he didn't have to go home. He didn't want to go back there ever again.

'Your mum and I have been talking,' Dad said, 'about getting away completely. Your mum suggested a holiday, a long holiday, but I don't think that will do.'

'So you mean moving?'

'I think it's the only way.'

'But where, where would we go? What about your business?'

'Well, technically I could set up anywhere,' Dad said, 'but it won't be easy to find new customers, the way the economy's going. And we might struggle to sell the house, of course.'

'But if we move,' said Shane, walking back towards the window, leaning against the sill, 'it's like admitting I did it, like saying I'm guilty.'

'We've thought of that,' Dad said. 'I mean I'm not even sure if we'd be allowed to leave the area just yet. But the solicitor's pretty sure there won't be any charges in the end.'

'So that'll prove it then,' said Shane. 'We won't need to move. Not right out of the area.'

But even as he said it he knew he was wrong. He knew he couldn't go back to school come

September, even if they'd let him. He couldn't face Ravi or Jackie or even people like Liam who said they believed him. He couldn't cope with them looking at him, wondering, thinking stuff. It wasn't fair. It wasn't bloody fair.

'We need to look into it a bit more,' his dad said. 'Your mum reckons we should—'

'Keep our options open?' said Shane.

'Yeah,' said Dad, trying to force a smile, 'how did you guess? We'll work something out, Shane, I promise. But first I'm going to grab a bit of breakfast, you coming? Your mum doesn't fancy any.'

'Not sure I do either. I might come down in a bit.'

He wasn't going to though, he had other things to do; two very important things.

'Can I borrow your phone?' he asked, as his dad stood up to leave.

'Why, what's wrong with yours?'

'Battery's down, didn't bring my charger.'

'OK,' said Dad. 'I'll be going over to the house later so make a list of anything you want picking up. Who are you calling?' he added, as he handed the phone over.

'Just a mate,' said Shane, 'one of the few I've got left.'

He waited until his dad left before tapping in the

231

number. He wasn't phoning a mate and there was nothing wrong with his own phone. He just needed to use one Lucy wouldn't recognise, one she'd probably answer. He knew it was mad but he needed to know. Before he left, before he made any decisions, he needed to know if it was true.

'Don't hang up,' he said as soon as he heard her voice. He wouldn't have long. She wouldn't exactly want to chat, so he needed to ask her straightaway. 'I just want to know if it's true what Jackie told me. Are you pregnant?'

There was a silence that seemed to last for ever.

'And why should I tell you?'

'You know why! Please, Lucy, just tell me, yes or no.'

But it was too late. Lucy had already gone. Shane threw Dad's phone down on the bed and turned to look out of the window again, vaguely in the direction of their old house, the school, the places he was going to have to leave. Why, why had Hannah done this to him? One thing was certain, he wasn't going anywhere until he'd found out from the only person who could tell him for sure. He took his own phone from the pocket of his jeans, made sure it was switched off, picked up his jacket and headed out.

28

Zak ate the toast and gulped down the coffee Dad had insisted on making for him.

'Gotta go,' he said, 'the boss is off today. I'm supposed to be in charge.'

'I didn't know he left you in charge. I mean, that's really good, Zak. He must trust you.'

'He does,' said Zak. 'Moans like hell at me, a bit like you really, but he says I'm a good worker – well, most of the time. Reckons I've got potential!'

He didn't tell his dad what else the boss said about how he thought Zak should go to college part-time, pick up some catering qualifications. It would only set his dad off again. Instead, Zak picked up his car keys off the table but put them down again as his phone beeped.

'Text from Lee,' he said.

'Lee Broadhurst?' Dad asked, managing to cram

all his feelings about Lee into the way he said the name.

'Yeah, I know, he's a total moron but he's a useful moron,' Zak said. 'He knows everythin' that's goin' on – usually before it even happens!'

For general information Zak used the net, like everyone else. Picking up the gossip about Lucy that Clare had tried to keep quiet or other fairly ordinary stuff, but for the special stuff he relied a lot on Lee.

'Look at this,' he said, handing his phone to Dad.

Dad peered at it then handed it straight back.

'I can't read it without my glasses and I can never make out text-speak anyway.'

'Yeah, 'specially when it's Lee. He can't bloody spell in any sort of language and he gets stuff all mixed up, but he's not done so bad with this.'

'Looks like a long message. What's he saying?'

'I asked him to find out who done that brick-lobbing. Just to prove to you and the boss that it weren't me.'

'I didn't think it was!' Dad insisted.

'Anyway he has. He reckons the cops have picked up a couple of lads for attacking Shane's house last night. Somebody saw 'em doing it. Then they got picked up on CCTV in the next street.'

'Does he say who it was?'

'No names but they're from the school. Year Tens, he reckons. I mean, what've they got to do with Shane or Hannah?'

'Probably nothing,' said Dad, 'they probably just did it for the hell of it. Any excuse. But I thought it happened on Wednesday night, not last night and it was the neighbour's house not Shane's. That's what you said.'

'Yeah, I know, and it was the neighbour, definitely. Lee might have got mixed up – wouldn't be the first time,' Zak said, scrolling down, trying to make out the rest of the message.

'Could be a separate incident,' said Dad, 'or the same kids coming back when they realised they'd got the wrong house first time round.'

'Oh shit,' said Zak, 'how the hell does Lee find out all this stuff?'

'What?' said Dad.

'Well if Lee's right and if those lads did do the old neighbour's place as well, they're in big, big trouble.'

He read the text to Dad before darting out. He glanced at his watch as he got in the car. He'd told Dad the truth, for once. The boss was away and he was in charge so he had to be early, but not quite this early. He drove the long route round, the very long route that took him past Hannah's, and stopped the car at the bottom of her drive. He couldn't see the house from there but, as he looked up the driveway, he saw a figure disappearing round the bend. Or at least he thought he did. Because he blinked and when he looked again the figure had gone.

It had looked like Shane but it couldn't have been because there was no way Shane would come back here. It was probably Hannah's dad, Zak decided, or more likely there was never anyone there at all, he'd probably imagined it. He hadn't heard any more freaky voices recently, but his head still didn't feel right after his bust up with Jed.

There was no more movement, no more activity, either real or imagined. So he just sat for a while, staring at the open gate, thinking about Hannah. He wanted her more than he'd ever done, wanted to help her, wanted to make things better. But he knew he couldn't, he could only make things worse. Hannah was right. With or without all this, it would never have worked out between them. It would be better to just drive away but somehow he couldn't. Not just yet. Something, he wasn't sure what, was keeping him there.

*

Hannah stood up when she heard the shouting. She'd been lying on Kyra's bed for most of the morning, watching one of her sister's stupid, cutesy Disney films. It was one of the DVDs Zak had brought back but she tried not to think about that. She tried not to think about anything except the cartoon animals bounding across the screen, singing their oh-so-jolly songs. She'd even laughed occasionally. Something that felt strangely forced, as if the laughter wasn't part of her at all.

'They're arguing again,' Kyra said, her voice flat, resigned.

'No,' said Hannah, 'they can't be. Dad's gone out. It's not Mum and Dad.'

'Well somebody's yelling,' Kyra said, getting up, stopping the film.

Hannah listened for a moment to see if she could make out the voices but she couldn't. She thought she'd heard the doorbell a few minutes ago but it was in the middle of some loud, bouncy scene so she couldn't be sure. Dad wouldn't ring the bell, he'd have his keys and besides, it really didn't sound like him.

She headed downstairs, closely followed by Kyra. The voices were coming from the kitchen. The door was open. She could see her mum and someone else. Mum's hands were held up as if she was trying to warn the other person away, push them back without actually touching them. Hannah moved forward slightly, trying to look past Mum. Then she saw him. It was Shane. Shane was standing right there in their bloody kitchen! What the hell was he doing here? Was he completely insane? Thank God Dad wasn't here, he'd have killed him. Instinctively she backed away, straight into Kyra, treading on her bare foot, making her yelp.

'Hannah!' Shane yelled, pushing past Mum.

Mum moved quicker than Hannah had ever seen her move. She grabbed Shane's arm, pulling him back, placing herself between Shane and the door.

'Hannah, Kyra, go back upstairs, now,' Mum said.

Hannah heard Kyra give a little screech before padding back towards the stairs, obedient as ever, but Hannah couldn't move.

'What's he doing here?' she asked Mum. 'Why did you let him in?'

'I didn't have much choice,' Mum said. 'Go upstairs, Hannah. Phone the police. He won't go. I need to get him out. I can't have him here when your dad gets back.'

'I don't care about him or the cops,' Shane said.

'I want to talk to Hannah. I want to know why you've done it,' he said, managing to look round Mum straight at Hannah.

He barely looked like Shane somehow. His face looked thinner, greyer, as if it belonged to a much older person. His forehead was all screwed up, his hair uncombed, his eyes half-closed.

'Why *she's* done it!' Mum screamed. 'Hannah hasn't done anything! How dare you come here, how dare you? This is harassment.'

'Harassment,' Shane snapped, 'yeah, right! You don't know nothing about bloody harassment. We've had phone calls, notes, messages sprayed on the walls. Bricks thrown through our windows and through our neighbour's window. Mrs Yates, she was eighty-six! You remember Mrs Yates, don't you, Hannah?'

Hannah felt a chill spreading down her arms at the use of the past tense. She started to shiver as Shane went on.

'She died last night. Have you got that? She's dead! Mrs Yates is dead. I found her lying on the floor. She'd had a heart attack cos of all the bloody stress. She died in the ambulance on the way to hospital. That's harassment,' he was shouting into Mum's face. 'She died cos of all this!'

The chill had turned to sudden burning heat. Hannah could feel the sweat on her face, her hands and her arms. She didn't know Shane's neighbour very well but she'd seen her often enough, usually on Sundays round at Shane's. She'd spoken to her, eaten slices of the fruitcake she'd made and yawned at her stories of the olden days. Was it her fault, was it all her fault that Mrs Yates had died, is that what Shane was saying?

'I'm sorry,' Mum said, edging away from Shane, nearer to Hannah. 'I'm sorry about your neighbour but it's got nothing to do with us. We didn't throw bricks through the windows.'

'You didn't have to,' Shane said, moving into the space Mum had left, staring at Hannah again.

'No,' Mum yelled, 'don't even think of blaming Hannah! You don't even know that the heart attack...I mean they can happen any time to anyone. You don't know that it's connected.'

'Yeah, right,' said Shane. 'That's what the cops said. We don't know that the bricks lobbed through her window were meant for us. It could have been a coincidence. And we can't prove that's what caused the heart attack. She was old, she was frail, she'd had some heart problems before. She might have died anyway, so that's fine then.'

'No, it's not fine,' said Mum, her voice, sharp, bitter, 'but if the attack came on because of the stress and if you're really looking for someone to blame, Shane, I suggest—'

She stopped as the phone rang. They all looked towards it but Hannah was nearest so she picked it up.

'Is he there?' a woman's voice said before Hannah had a chance to speak. 'Is Shane there? Please tell me I'm wrong. Please tell me he's not there.'

Hannah knew it was Kim, Shane's mum, but she didn't sound quite like Kim because nobody looked or sounded the same any more. It was like living in some bizarre parallel universe where nothing was right, wouldn't ever be right again.

'Yes, he's here,' Hannah managed to say.

'Oh, God, I knew it,' Kim said. 'His dad said he might have run away but I knew he wouldn't do that. I told you,' she added, talking to someone in the room with her, Shane's dad probably. 'I knew that's where he'd gone. I knew it. Can I speak to him? I need to talk to him. Is he all right?'

Kim's voice sounded so strange, like she was in pain, physical pain. Hannah held the phone out to where Shane and her mum were standing. She didn't know what else to do.

'It's Kim,' she told her mum, 'she wants to talk to Shane.'

Mum moved away from the door automatically, letting Shane through. He snatched the phone from Hannah. He stood listening. Hannah could hear the buzz of his mum's voice going on and on, but she couldn't make out what Kim was saying. Hannah looked at her own mum, searching for answers, wondering what they should do. But Mum didn't seem to know either. Mum had got her mobile out but she wasn't using it, not yet.

'Yeah, all right, yeah,' Shane said at last, before putting the phone down. 'Mum says I have to leave,' he said. 'They're gonna come and pick me up.'

But he showed no sign of moving.

'Your mother's right,' Hannah's mum said, looking down at her mobile, 'because if you don't leave right now I'm calling the police.'

Shane didn't answer her. Instead he half-turned and looked at Hannah. She'd moved away from him when he'd put the phone down but he didn't look angry or dangerous. He looked scared, bemused, defeated.

'You know I didn't do it,' he said, shaking his head slightly. 'You must know what went on. You must remember! Hannah, look at me. I couldn't do that, you know I couldn't!'

Hannah looked. She hadn't stopped looking at him. He believed it. He really believed that she'd agreed, that she'd wanted to. Part of her almost wanted to lie now. To say she'd made a mistake, but she couldn't because it was all flooding back into her head. The moment when she'd said no, when she'd tried to push him away and he hadn't listened, he hadn't cared, he probably hadn't even bloody noticed.

She glanced at Mum, whose eyes moved from her to Shane and back again.

'Oh God,' Mum said.

And Hannah knew what Mum was seeing, what she was thinking, even before Mum moved towards them, even before she spoke.

'You could both do it, couldn't you?' she said. 'You could both look me in the eyes and swear you're telling the truth.'

'He's not though!' Hannah screamed. 'How can you believe him and not me?'

'That's not what I'm saying,' Mum murmured, shaking her head.

Hannah knew that; she knew what Mum was really saying. How it must look to anyone on the outside. Two drunken, drugged-up kids who didn't know what the hell they were doing. That's what the police thought, that's what any court would think, but it wasn't going to get that far.

'They're not gonna prosecute, you know,' Shane said, voicing her thoughts. 'They can't. There's no evidence. It's just your word against mine and even your own bloody mum isn't sure!'

'*She* might not be but I am!' Hannah screamed. 'Get out, just get out, leave me alone.'

She slumped back, using the wall for support. She knew he was right. There wasn't going to be a prosecution. It probably wouldn't even get as far as the CPS. They'd both got confused, lied about stuff somewhere along the way; no court would believe either of them.

'You can put that away,' Shane said to Mum as she started tapping a number into her phone. 'I'm going. And don't worry, I won't come back – not here, not to school.'

He headed towards the back door then paused, looking around.

'You won't be able to stay here, neither,' he said. 'You know that, don't you? You've screwed things up for both of us, Hannah.'

He looked as though he might be about to say

something else, but they all heard a noise. The sound of a car out the front then Kyra yelping from the top of the stairs, 'Dad's back.'

Hannah felt herself sliding down, slumping to the floor as Shane left out the back, and a few minutes later Dad walked in the front.

'What the hell's happened now?' he said, kneeling beside Hannah.

'Shane came,' said Kyra, heading downstairs.

Dad stood up again.

'Leave it,' Mum said, putting her hand on his arm. 'He's gone, it's all right.'

Hannah shuddered, another cold phase taking over from the heat. *All right – as if!* She looked at her parents and at Kyra with her split lip and the bruise round her jaw. Shane was right. They couldn't stay here now, no way. Her parents had already talked about moving even before they knew about what people were saying out in the park and online. It wouldn't be easy. They'd have to sell the house, find new jobs. That's why Mum had popped into work yesterday, to talk about a transfer and Dad was pretty confident he'd find something wherever they moved to.

Mum's boss had said there was something going in the Watford branch, not too far from Auntie

Paula's and Uncle Phil's. They could stay with them for a while, Auntie Paula had said. It wasn't ideal. Kyra would hate moving away from her friends. Gran would miss them, unless she decided to move too, but no way could they stay around here. This part of their lives was over. Shane was right about one thing. She'd ruined everything for all of them.

*

Zak sat up straight, his eyes fixed on Hannah's drive where a blue car had turned in about five minutes earlier. He'd slunk down in his seat as it passed; hoping Hannah's dad wouldn't see his car. It couldn't have been him he'd seen on the drive earlier. And, if it wasn't imagination, if it was who he'd originally thought it was, Zak knew there could be serious trouble.

The trouble appeared a few seconds later when Shane ran down the drive, looked left, saw Zak's car, saw Zak and belted off down the road to the right. Before Zak could even think about following, think about doing anything, a van appeared. It pulled into the side. Shane scrambled into the back then the van swung round and pulled away.

Zak stared like he was watching a scene from some crazy film, wondering what was going on and what Shane was doing there. He wondered where

Hannah was, whether she was OK and whether he should head up to the house and check. He clutched the edge of the seat with both hands, taking deep breaths, determined that he was going to stay in control. He wasn't going to let the blackness swallow him up, not this time.

Whatever had been going on, Hannah's dad was there now. Zak knew he should do what Clare said, not get involved. Even if Hannah was right there in the house, she was a million miles away from him now. Maybe, he reflected, she always had been. He felt the tears burning the back of his eyes, switched on the engine and drove away.

Epilogue

They'd done what they'd planned. They'd moved to Watford, and that's where Hannah had spent the last five years, slowly getting her life back. She'd eventually done her A levels, working for a while in various part-time jobs to rebuild her confidence. And now, just as she thought it was all behind her, just as she'd begun to move on, he was here. Zak – the very last person she'd expected to see at a university of any sort.

'Hannah,' Zak was saying, 'don't go.'

She stood, staring at him, unable to speak.

'Come and sit down,' he urged, 'just for a minute.'

She followed him to the table. It seemed the easiest option, somehow, with her legs threatening to give way at any minute.

'I can't believe it,' he said.

'Me neither,' she managed to say as she sat down.

She looked at the book that was lying open on the table.

'Business and Economics,' Zak said. 'I'm in my second year. I'm classed as a mature student, would you believe? Not sure what I'm gonna do when I've finished,' he said, talking fast as if he was scared of silences. 'I've got some catering qualifications from college and scraped enough points to get in here. You?'

'English,' she said.

She could have told him more but it seemed crazy talking about ordinary things like courses.

'I wanted to get in touch,' Zak said, 'for months after you left. But nobody knew where you'd gone and I sort of knew I couldn't anyway. I mean, I won't now. I can keep out of your way. It's a big place.'

'The world's a big place,' said Hannah, 'but sometimes it's not big enough. There's always going to be the chance of seeing someone, meeting someone.'

'I'm sorry,' said Zak, shuffling as if he was going to get up.

'No, I didn't just mean this, you. The bloody past follows you everywhere. You can't ignore it so you have to deal with it. That's what my counsellors used to tell me anyway.'

'Mine too,' said Zak. He paused, looking slightly embarrassed. 'Dad finally got me into therapy. Spent a fortune so I could learn to say I miss her. I miss my mum. See, I can do it now. And after a while it stops hurting so much.'

'Everything does,' said Hannah. 'You don't believe it will but it does.

'You still live with your dad, then,' she added, when he didn't comment, 'in the holidays and stuff?'

'Yeah but he lives in Leeds now with his new lady-friend. Someone he met on the bloody Internet!' Zak smiled that same amazing smile she remembered; the one that used to get him massive tips from his customers at the café. 'And if you knew my dad, you'd know just how bloody weird that was.'

'You OK with it though?'

'Yeah, I guess. It's his life and she's all right, I suppose. Not his type but then the strangest things work out sometimes.'

'Do they?'

Was it a hint? Was he talking about them?

'Yeah, I guess,' said Zak. 'I mean, do you remember Eden? Yeah, sorry, course you do. Well, er, I don't know whether I should be talking about this, you probably don't want to know.'

'No, go on, it's OK.'

'Well, she married that cop.'

'Bloody hell!' Hannah yelled, causing people to look towards her again.

'Yeah, God knows how she got round him after all that crap on the Internet but they got back together, got married, had a kid and they're still doin' all right as far as I know. Weird innit?'

It was way beyond weird. That relationship had seemed pretty unbelievable in the first place and it just didn't seem possible that it had survived all the business with Shane. She rubbed her arms, feeling suddenly cold. Did she really want to be straying back into this sort of territory, dredging it all up? Or should she go on just to prove she could?

'So you're still in touch with people from back then?' she asked.

'No, not really but I hear stuff sometimes, usually from Lee. He's still around. Got himself a job last I heard – so miracles do happen!'

'So do you know about anyone else? I mean like Lucy, did she— I mean, I know she was pregnant.'

'No,' said Zak, 'no, she wasn't. Jackie put the rumour round. Lucy didn't bother to deny it for ages but it was all bollocks.'

Hannah nodded, wondering whether she should ask about anyone else, whether she really wanted to know. Like her, they'd probably all moved on with their lives – even Shane. He'd be somewhere, living a normal life, as if none of it had ever happened – maybe thinking about it sometimes or maybe not. Probably still believing that she'd consented, that he'd done nothing wrong.

'But like I said,' Zak went on, 'I don't really bother with none of them much now. I won't tell anyone I've seen you or nothing. I mean, I'll keep out of your way if that's what you want. I promise.'

He looked at her and smiled again.

'But if you thought we could be like – friends . . . ' he said.

Hannah looked at him. He still talked the same, looked the same. He didn't seem to have aged much in five years, he was still totally fit, but he'd changed. They'd both changed. Could she hack it though, could she cope with someone from the past in her life? Would he eventually start asking questions, wanting to talk about the details of that night?

But then, with or without Zak around, it would all still be there. You couldn't ever alter the past. *Acknowledge it, learn to understand it, deal with it and move on.* That's what the counsellors had said.

'That's all I mean,' said Zak, his eyes all sort of soft and misty, 'just friends, nothing else.'

Hannah breathed in deeply like her therapist had taught her, then she smiled.

'Yes,' she said. 'I think we could be friends.'